BLOOD
CYPRESS

Published by Raw Dog Screaming Press
Bowie, MD
First Edition

Cover art copyright 2024 by Lynne Hansen
LynneHansenArt.com
Book Design by Jennifer Barnes

Printed in the United States of America

ISBN: 978-1-947879-88-1

Library of Congress Control Number:
2025930091

RawDogScreaming.com

BLOOD CYPRESS

ELIZABETH BROADBENT

RAW DOG
SCREAMING
PRESS

For David, Raven, and Toci

Southern Histories

I have never been able to fully detach, rest, recuperate or…whatever trendy euphemism for "taking a break from work" is currently in favor. Thus, it should be no surprise I am checking in and making an entry here during what is supposed to be my sabbatical.

Yes, this academia approved time is technically for working on special projects related to our disciplines, only without the additional tasks of emails, meetings, course development/rendering, and grading. My official proposal sought approval to work on an essay about the importance of not only welcoming oral stories and histories into the academy as credible sources in humanities studies, but the necessity of the foundations the histories provide. I am building on the work of oral history scholars such as historian Allan Nevins and revolutionary Bell Hooks.

Just as I headed down home to Texas to work in a plantation's extensive archives, I detoured through South Carolina and what started out as a temporary stop suddenly became a much-needed examination into the Carson family, of Eliza Broadbent's paper, Blood Cypress. Not only am I excited to incorporate some themes from Broadbent's paper into my own research, but I am also looking forward to investigating more fellow Southerners' history.

A lifelong Southerner until I joined my current university—the Selected Papers from the Consortium for the Study of Anomalous Phenomena would likely not exist in the open in a Southern institution—I needed no further explanation of Broadbent's description of the swamp surrounding the Carson homestead as smelling like "sweet rot". The existence of sweetness and putrescence simultaneously is a distinctly Southern trait. This descriptor can be applied to almost anything in this culture: the food, attitudes, practices, and lineage.

Lineage and family are foundational to Southerners, no matter how sweetly rotten that foundation might be. Familial lines full of cracks, mold, and decay permeate the beauteous South, covered delicately by the breezes blowing through the shadows of huge oak trees and the protection of lush Spanish moss providing refuge for ugliness. The blanket of steamy humidity completes the disguising of the cracks genteel

Southerners do not want discovered.

The Carson family lived under such secrecy. Their pretty mother had not been born for work, but for breeding and ornamental value. Upon the death of her husband, their oldest son, Davis, attempted to keep the household in order, as their mother descended into the helplessness of frailty. This is what the eldest sons of the South did. The middle twins, Quentin and Lila, have been allowed, albeit, barely, to skirt the familial expectation that may have been otherwise bestowed on them through their pursuit of education and insistence on living as freely as they are able.

When the youngest son, Beau, goes missing, the biggest detriment to Southern delusions of grandeur is exposed: unyielding secrecy in the face of keeping up proper appearances. The Carson family understands Beau is different from the rest of them and his differences do not escape the young child, himself. He needs special care, however, to yield to that need would require exposing him and the failing of their blood to the ever-judgmental townsfolk. Keeping Beau and the family reputation "safe" at home sets the Carson family on an unavoidable course towards retribution and destruction. Secrets require payment and Broadbent describes the ultimate cost of these surreptitious events with decadently lyrical Southern gothic storytelling that has earned its place as an installment in our department archives.

The discovery of this Southern family narrative will also require a little longer term on my sabbatical. Perhaps uncovering more secrets will help me commune with the swamp in paying homage to other Southern histories...after all, I may have a little blood of the cypress in me, too.

By Dr. Calixta Beauregard

CHAPTER ONE

The girl on Vickery's corner barstool drank alone. Darkness drew her in sharp shadows; when her short bob wasn't falling in her face, she gave off a Kate Moss-ish air, all wide eyes and high cheekbones. Eleven o'clock had struck and passed. I liked risk, and I liked girls steeped in mysterious sadness. "Send her a drink," I told the bartender.

"She's throwing down top-shelf bourbon." He swiped his hands on a white towel. "Don't shell out for that."

The girl stared at her glass as if it offered truth or wisdom or at least oblivion; her pink State Champs shirt, black arm warmers, and black beanie said pop-punk kid, maybe late-stage emo girl. "Send it anyway," I said.

He poured her drink, then tipped his head toward me. She snapped up and peered down the bar.

"If you're ordering my bourbon, come sit with me." The girl spoke, her voice thick with liquor and the South. "It's been a long time."

A long time since someone had bought her a drink? Hard to believe, with her looks. A long time since she'd drank with another woman, maybe, or a long time since she'd drank with anyone at all? I slipped from my stool. "McKenzie Newcomb," I said, smoothing my black dress under me as I sat.

Her smile passed like a ghost. "Y'all Yankees. No time for how are you or it's late or isn't it cold tonight? I'm Lila Carson, lately from Lower Congaree, South Carolina. Don't worry, you've never heard of it." She drained one drink and sipped her next. "Where're you from, McKenzie Newcomb?"

"Manhattan."

"That's a quick train ride. Lemme guess." She pursed her lips a bit—pretty lips, full and pouty. Light and dark played over her face. "You did St. Mark's, didn't you?"

"Close. Phillips Exeter. What brought you to Princeton?"

"Long story." Lila drank again. "What kept you here?"

"I don't know. You stay here, I guess."

We went silent for a few beats, as if we'd run out of words. Lovely pink stains lined Lila's glass. "Do you miss it?" I asked. "On nights like this, with fall and everything. You must miss it."

She didn't speak for a long time. "I miss decent biscuits. You miss the food, mostly, other than the heat. The heat's a whole 'nother story."

"What do you mean?"

"It swallows you, and you love it 'cause you can't fight it. You can say that about a lot of things down there." She contemplated her bourbon again.

"What's it like?"

Lila laughed suddenly, a low laugh but a long one. "The small-town South is its own animal, and it's still feral."

"I've been to the Outer Banks," I offered.

"Yankee vacation outpost," she said. "Doesn't count."

"It can't be that horrible, though," I said.

11

Her gaze caught mine. She had blue eyes and a slow, feline blink. "It's worse," she replied.

"But you escaped."

"You could call it that." She leaned on her elbows, and I resisted a sudden urge to pet her arm. For all her sharp angles and long lines, she hinted at a pliable softness. "Yeah," she said. "You could say I escaped."

"How'd you do that?" I asked.

"Long story."

"Do you have anything better to do tonight?"

"The bourbon says I should ask you to come home." Glancing down and nibbling her bottom lip, Lila could've been playing shy. But I read something different there: I'd like to hook up, but I'm telling you how I'd like it to go. "You bought me a drink, it's late, and you seem like a good listener."

"Those are good reasons." I wanted to pull her dark hair and kiss that sadness away. "Let's talk about it while we walk to your place. But I'm texting my friends your address in case you're a serial killer." Lila as a serial killer: laughable. She seemed more likely to save a spider rather than swat it. I opened my purse, tipped my chin at the bartender, and held out my card. "Cash me out, please."

Lila touched my hand. "Put her drinks on my tab, please, Stephen." She stood—a bit taller than me, but we'd even out once she ditched those pink Doc Martens. With heart-shaped buckles, they hit both punk and cute, like her shirt. I zipped my card into my wallet and shut my purse. Lila bundled on a thermal hoodie.

"What?" Her arched brows met when I laughed.

"Your insulated hoodie. It's chilly, but it's not cold."

She pulled on a pair of fuzzy pink mittens. "It's freezing out."

"What will you do when real winter comes?"

"Curl up in a ball and hibernate til spring." She spoke so seriously that I almost believed her. "But c'mon, it's close," Lila said, and led me into the night.

CHAPTER TWO

A long time later, Lila stared at her ceiling. Old lamps yellowed her dark hair, which spilled messily over mounded pillows. We lay on a four-poster canopied bed, under a hand-stitched quilt unraveled into broken threads. Her pinkish Persian rug frayed; expensive makeup scattered a tasseled vanity. Those touches shouted old money and lots of it. She yawned. "You're sweet, McKenzie. I haven't done that in a long time."

Well, why the hell not? I wanted to ask. Time had left her lace-edged sheets silky, and under them, she was all long, lovely softness. I was torn between snuggling her warmth and slipping down those sheets just to look. "It was good," I replied. "You pay attention."

"I try." She still stared at her ceiling. "So why has it been a long time?"

"You ask a lot of questions." A smile hid in her tone.

"Because you wouldn't talk if I didn't." I ran a hand through her hair. "Tell me I'm wrong."

"No, you're probably right." She didn't speak for a few moments, as if she were weighing her words. "I don't know what to say a lot of the time, so I don't say anything at all. I can't believe I asked you to come home with me." She laughed a little. "That was definitely the bourbon."

"For the record, I'm glad you asked."

"Me too," Lila said, but she lapsed into silence again. She seemed remote, as if she'd become accustomed to keeping a certain distance from others and she wasn't sure how to breach it.

I could've curled around her, but instead, I propped myself on an elbow. "Tell me why you came to Princeton."

"You really want to hear it?" Her Southern drawl seemed poignant and broken. "You won't believe it."

"I'll believe it."

Lila's eyes didn't leave that white ceiling. Its popcorning crumbled in places; fine dust clung to her bedside tables. "No. I mean you literally won't believe it." She flipped on her side. "But it happened."

"I'll believe you." I'd have promised her anything then.

"You won't," Lila said. "But I'll tell you anyway."

Chapter Three

2016

"I have to run to Hopkins," Mama said.

That's Hopkins General Store on Main Street, and they keep Lower Congaree in everything from baby shoes to baking soda. If we wanted Walmaart we drove over twenty miles to Gaston. Lower Congaree's what we called the ass-end of nowhere—BFE, for bumfuck Egypt. I used that phrase at a party up here in Princeton, and they started a huge argument: was that a gay slur or Orientalism? I tried to tell them it was only a thing we said, like fuck a duck doesn't mean you wanna bang the mallards. I said it didn't mean a damn thing. No one listened.

Then I thought that sometimes they said buttfuck Egypt instead, and I realized I was wrong. It's all there. You live in it so long you don't see it. We're born blind, and when some start to see its hazy edges they snap their eyes shut from fear. Some open their eyes wider, and they either stay to fix it or run as far and as fast as they can.

When Mama said she had to run out, Quentin, Davis, and I were eating sandwiches I'd grabbed at the Gas N Go. Beau had picked his apart, eaten what he wanted, and wandered off to play. Mama didn't eat lunch so she leaned against the kitchen counter. Quentin and I had a study group at school, and we were leaving soon. Davis knew it, and he also knew Mama was sideways asking him for help, since she didn't like to take Beau out alone.

We were eighteen years old then, Quentin and me. Davis was a junior at Carolina, and Beau was ten. Mama always said she had Beau late, and late babies were more likely to come out wrong. That's how she said it, come out wrong, and she didn't mean anything cruel, but it didn't matter 'cause everyone heard it, Beau included. It was a long, long time before I thought about those words, how they shaped my world, and how they shaped Beau's. How they shaped Lower Congaree even, those words coming again and again like our swamp water seeps in and out.

See, Lower Congaree lies on and through and around one of the largest tracts of uncut old-growth forest in the eastern US. You know they're bragging when they call it forest. They don't say no one logged it 'cause it's swampland, and I don't mean swampland like it's muddy. I mean water there rises and falls with the Congaree River. That water sours with tannin—that's why we call it blackwater swamp—then sits stagnant in sloughs and guts and pools. There's a certain scent to it— rich, ripe dirt but silt left out to rot, too. I came up in that, and when I was little I thought the whole world smelled like slow, sweet decay.

But there's something else.

Stand on the edge of that swamp, right where water and land become uncertain brothers, and that soupy air turns scum-sweet. Gaze back into those cypresses that seem old as bones. The distance goes gray and dim even when the sun shines. There'll be cicadas shrieking and mosquitoes buzzing, but under it all you'll hear the quiet. You'll feel it then. The hair on your neck will rise, and you'll know it's watching. You'll know it's waiting, too, and if you step wrong it'll suck you down into that muck with every other lost thing. It was there before us, and it'll be there after. That's the real reason they never cut that swampland.

We stayed away from it. That was part of living in Lower Congaree: you stayed out of the swamp, and you left it to its business, whatever that may be. We warned Beau off it over and over—tried to scare him silly with stories about the evil things that lurked there. I wondered later if he understood. He did, of course. Beau heard everything and understood everything. I know that now.

Women were always sighing over Beau. Why'd God waste those long lashes on a boy, they'd say, or, Why'd God give a boy those pretty curls? Everyone in town swore we Carson kids looked just like Mama, and she was Miss Legare County. We all had her big blue eyes, but only Beau got her curls. Miz Leonard always called him a changeling, and she said that's why he didn't talk.

"He doesn't need to talk," I told her when I was fourteen. I had him in my arms and I cuddled him closer. "He can never talk for the rest of his life and it doesn't matter."

"Caroline Candice!" Mama snatched up Beau. He started to cry and reach for me.

"Well he doesn't!" I said.

"You apologize to Miz Leonard right now!" Mama told me.

I glared at Mama. Beau kept crying. I'd cut my long hair not a week before.

Miz Leonard seemed to examine Mama. She turned a beady-eyed look on Beau, then on me. "Blood tells," she said, and shuffled off. Mama wanted to beat my ass that night, and she would've if she wasn't so busy crying.

"You see what you did?" Davis asked. We stood in the third-floor hallway. Mama was sobbing in her room. "You had to go and chop off all your hair and now this. You know what they say about us in town, and you don't help any."

"Don't you raise your voice at me." I kept my tone polite 'cause I didn't wanna upset Beau. He already had his hands over his ears.

"Will y'all please just stop?" Quentin said. "Lila can cut her hair if she wants."

"You only say that 'cause you grow yours out," Davis told him. "You know what you look like, don't you? You know what they say about y'all two?"

Quentin walked away.

"He might not look it in the face but you will," Davis told me.

"Maybe I don't care." I shifted Beau to my other hip.

"Maybe you should," Davis snapped. "And maybe I do. Maybe Quentin does, too, but he won't say it 'cause he loves you."

I left Davis alone outside of Mama's room.

By the time Beau was ten, he'd grown too big to carry like that, so Mama didn't wanna take him out alone. I don't mean he weighed much—Beau was a skinny thing, but he was the same height as any ten-year-old boy. When he was smaller, if he wanted to stay somewhere too long or go someplace we didn't, Quentin or Mama or me would scoop him up. Time to go, Beau, we'd say, all fake-cheerful, like he couldn't tell the difference. He might cry and twist in our arms, but not for long. It made me sad to see how fast he'd go quiet, like he knew he wouldn't get what he wanted and he might as well not fight for it. But I never asked questions. We did the best we could.

It wasn't good enough. It wasn't good enough at all.

So when Mama had to go to the store, she didn't want to take Beau alone. She worried he'd start watching something and he wouldn't want to leave, or that the people and the noise, the colors and the smells would overwhelm him. Then sometimes he would cry and scream and make a scene. Mama couldn't stand scenes. She worried if she took Beau she might as well not bother going.

"Davis, can you come with us?" she asked.

"Can't Lila go?" he said. "I've got work to do."

"Lila says she and Quentin have things to do at school," Mama told him.

"I don't have time to fool around," Davis said. "Wait til they get back."

"By then Hopkins'll be closed."

"I don't know what you need so bad that you need to go now."

"Davis, will you please just watch him here then?" Mama asked, and her voice went higher 'cause she didn't know what to do with him telling her no when she needed something. Davis didn't want to set her off, so he went quiet and Mama got her way.

Quentin and I got ready to leave. Beau watched me tie my Doc Martens and I kissed his head. "Be good," I said. "I love you. But I'm going to school and you can't come."

He sat on the couch and pulled his knees to his chest. Since that summer I'd worried Beau thought we didn't want him. I was scared he woke hollow-chested and carried it all day, sunk-in and lonely. He didn't go anywhere and he had no one but us. Mama saying he needed to sleep alone scared me. I knew that feeling. I hadn't before, 'cause I'd always had Quentin, but then I didn't—or if I did it wasn't the same, it would never be the same—and there's nothing worse than being alone. I really think it's the worst thing in the world, and you can tell life to fuck off through anything else. But if you're alone, you stop caring.

I made sure to kiss him one more time. "I love you more than the whole entire world," I said.

Beau didn't like to look at people's faces, so he nodded at the floor. That was his way.

"You understand that, right?" I asked.

He nodded again.

"I'll be home soon," I said. "I love you, I love you, I love you." Beau was too big, but I picked him up and hugged him anyway. He hung on tight, and he didn't want me to put him down. Beau sat on the couch again. Mama had already gone.

Davis twisted his mouth as Quentin and I passed through the kitchen. "You just have to wear those boots, don't you?"

"Fuck off," I said.

"You know what they say about you," he told me.

"You can fuck right off to sunny California."

He made a noise in his throat. "You know what you look like in those boots and jeans and that tank top, he said. Listening to that stupid music. Why don't you act like a goddamn girl for once?"

Quentin grabbed my hand and dragged me out. He hated when Davis and I fought.

So we left, and Davis stayed with Beau. Beau never liked Davis much. Beau could be stubborn, and he wouldn't listen if he thought you didn't care one way or another. He was like anyone else, y'know? That's where everything went wrong. Beau was different, but he wasn't different at all. I wonder sometimes if—but there's no good in that. You could lose yourself in wondering. Wonder too far and you'll fall off the edge of the world. Mama used to say that, and it's true. You can lose a life in what-ifs.

Davis was studying accounting at the university, and he'd come home that weekend with a briefcase full of work. He hated it, but he said someone had to learn enough to keep up the place, and that someone had to be him. "Mama can't do it," he'd told Quentin and me that summer. "You know Mama can't do it. It'll go to ruin if she tries much longer."

Quentin left. Trust Quentin to walk away when you said something he didn't want to hear.

"What d'you mean it'll go to ruin?" I asked.

Davis's mouth turned into a thin line. "You can be an idiot, Lila, but you're not blind," he said. "You think everything's okay? You think she's okay?"

"That doesn't mean—" I started.

"You think you're gonna do it?" He laughed. "Without me and Quentin they'd say you were a hero for it. But you got two brothers, and if we don't they'll ask why we let you do it instead, and what d'you think that'll say about us?"

I pressed my lips together. We both knew what they'd say about it.

"What d'you think they'll say about you, too?" Davis's eyes narrowed and turned mean. He always knew exactly how to make people do what he wanted.

I shut up.

Quentin and I went to our study group. Beau stayed home with Davis. We left around one in the afternoon, then came back at three. When Quentin pulled in the drive, Mama and Davis stood in front of the house. Mama's eyes were wide and scared, and dust covered her dress—Mama never walked out the front door without everything perfect. She put on makeup to walk to the mailbox. You know those women. You hurt for them if you think too hard. Davis didn't seem scared. He had that tight-mouthed look he got when he did something wrong and didn't want to tell.

"Something's not right," Quentin said as he threw the car into park.

I looked from Mama to Davis, then around our weedy yard. Quentin needed to mow it, but you can only do so many things in a day, and if anyone bitched, well, they didn't understand that our days were real goddamn full. Davis wouldn't've left his schoolwork unless something terrible happened, and there weren't many terrible things left to happen by then.

"Where's Beau?" I asked. My heart beat like a fist squeezed it. "I don't see Beau."

I was out of that car and into the drive as fast as I could go, Quentin right behind me.

"Where's Beau?" Quentin asked.

"We checked everywhere inside twice," Mama told us. "We can't find him. Davis says he might be playing a game—"

"Beau doesn't play games like that!" I said, mostly to Davis 'cause he knew better. "You think he plays stupid games?"

"He might." Mama twisted her fingers together. "Davis says—"

"Oh, if Davis says it, it must be true," I shot back. "He doesn't even know where Beau likes to hide."

Quentin and I ran into the house. "If you sound scared, he'll be scared and he won't come out," I said. "Maybe they sounded scared and that's why he's hiding, so we have to pretend we're playing hide and seek."

Quentin started in the attic and I started at the front door. "Come out, come out, wherever you are," I called. "Beau, come out, the game's over and you won." I used my sweetest voice, and I checked everywhere. Under the armchairs, behind the refrigerators. I checked places a skinny ten-year-old probably couldn't climb, like up the chimney. I think I flipped the couch cushions.

When Quentin and I met in the middle of the second-floor hallway, he had that same wide-eyed, scared look as Mama. "Beau's not in the house," he said. "Mama's gonna lose her goddamn mind."

He'd never said it before. We might've been twins but we didn't mention some things, especially not then, and one of them was Mama. Maybe when Daddy died, she couldn't stand to look at the world anymore. Or maybe it was a slow kind of slide—they made her into Miss Legare County and they made her into a wife, and after that they had nothing else to make her, so she haunted our house on the edge of the swamp like a beautiful gray-eyed ghost.

Daddy died when Quentin and me were eleven. Mama was a Burr—the Burrs didn't arrive til after Reconstruction, and if you got someone drunk enough they'd call them carpetbaggers, 'cause old families in Lower Congaree, they'd still say things like that, and they'd still lead to fistfights. She might've been Miss Legare County, but after Daddy passed she didn't keep up the tobacco, or even the hay fields, so she had to fire the staff. Then she couldn't keep up the house, so she closed off the fourth floor. She didn't keep up repairs 'cause she didn't have a handyman around. So when Beau turned out the way he did, and I was running around with short hair in my brother's shirts, they thought she couldn't keep up her kids, either.

She managed Beau while we were at school 'cause he was quiet. He'd watch his animal documentaries or play with his toys, and Quentin or me would make sure to leave some kinda lunch she could hand him, a sandwich or leftovers to heat up. We'd even set an alarm for one o'clock to tell her to feed him, 'cause otherwise she'd forget. Then after school, she'd sort of drift away. We learned to cook real fast.

The year Daddy died, of course, Quentin and I didn't show up at cotillion—that's the special manners class kids take in middle school. You learn what fork to use and how to waltz. They still have debutante balls down there, and you damn well better know how to waltz when you come out. I don't mean come out of the closet, either. But when we didn't show up at cotillion the year after that, people started to talk. This was even before I cut my hair. You should put her in pageants, they'd tell Mama. And she'd say, That's for Lila to decide, which they'd take to mean she was too lazy to make me. I thought that was the reason then too, even if I thanked God for it, but now I wonder. I really do.

I'd thought Quentin and I would find Beau in the house, but when we didn't, I got real scared. "Well, he'd never go in the big barn," I said. "You know how he feels about those mowers. And he wouldn't stay in a shed 'cause the dust makes him sneeze and he hates the tobacco smell. We have to go outside."

I knew then. I knew it with everything in me. Beau had changed sometime around the middle of that summer. Quentin would ask him to walk down to the Wishing Well, and he'd shake his head. I'd say, Beau, let's go look for some flowers. He'd curl up with his knees to his chest and duck his head between them. He turned to the wall when we talked to him, and he stopped watching his nature documentaries. He sat by the window a lot. Whatcha looking at, Quentin or me would ask. He'd act like we hadn't spoken.

"He's sad, Mama," I said one night. "You should take Beau to the doctor."

Her head whipped up. She met my eyes, and hers were fiercer than I'd ever seen them. "No doctors," she told me, and that was the end.

You could stand in the middle of our land and smell that sweet-rot. On every side, vines tangled, and bald cypress and swamp tupelo shouldered up from those first muddy seepings. Beyond them, you'd see nothing but an indistinguishable gray. You might think about what was back there, but it was a kind of worrying, not wondering.

Men go in that swamp and don't come out. I mean seasoned hunters, guys with tactical gear and AR-15s and real wood sense. They vanish. I heard Discovery Channel tried to make a special about that once and couldn't. But you hear so many things living out there. It's hard to sift truth from rumor, and rumor from chatter, and chatter from outright lies. There's malice and there's gossip and there's those who don't know better. They're all different.

When Quentin and I came out of the house, Sheriff Irwin and his deputies were parking in the drive. Legare County's sheriff had nothing to do but sit on his ass and wait for something to happen. Hardly anything happened. The Joiners or the Leonard boys might cook up meth, but the sheriff only bothered them if they were real obvious or had kids around. Sheriff Irwin showed up with the whole force not 'cause they cared but 'cause they had jackshit else going on.

The sheriff climbed out of his patrol car slow, like he didn't need to hurry. Then he hitched up his pants. You could tell a Legare

County cop by his belly, since they spent their all time eating at Brewster's Diner or drinking at the Backdoor Bar. While Sheriff Irwin yanked his pants he looked up at our house. I was eighteen and I understood he was taking in whatever he could carry back to town. He'd plop his ass on a stool at the diner or the bar and say to whoever was listening, Well I got called up to the Carsons' and did you know.

That's how it was.

"Heard your boy's missing, Miz Carson," Sheriff Irwin finally said, like he didn't care the whole damn family was standing at the head of our drive, like Mama wasn't shaking and Quentin wasn't holding her hand.

Davis stood a little way off with his arms crossed. He had that drawn-in, tense look he got sometimes since Daddy died. Davis never told me—Davis never told me anything—but I think Daddy gave him that oldest-son speech, that speech that says you're the man of the house, you take care of your mama and brothers and sister when I'm gone. It was that oldest son thing—why do you think he was Jefferson Davis Carson IV?

An heir and a spare and a girl for Mama, Daddy used to say. Your mama did good.

Well, what's Beau, I always wanted to ask. Quentin can be the spare and I can be for Mama, but Beau should be something too. Beau didn't count 'cause he didn't talk and he couldn't stand loud noises and crowds. But Daddy would've said the same thing Mama did: Beau was born wrong. That boy ain't right, that's what people in Lower Congaree would've told you. That was like using the R-word, but they'd still say it.

I bet Beau could've gone to school. I bet we could've figured out how. They say Yankees keep their crazy aunts in the attic, but Southerners bring her down to tea. That sounds real funny, but no one says anything about letting her out. And no one says anything about her feelings on the matter, either.

Mama was crying too hard to talk. "Beau's never been anywhere by himself," I told Sheriff Irwin. "He never even played outside by himself."

"Are you Quentin or Caroline Candice?" he asked, and he said it with a straight face, too. "I can't ever tell you two apart."

He damn well could tell us apart. My hair was a little above my chin—I never had it any shorter. Quentin might've had his the same length, but I was clearly a girl with a bob, and he looked like a boy with chin-length hair. He had an Adam's apple, for God's sake. But the sheriff's deputies glanced down and grinned or snorted back laughter. The sheriff's question said everything about who we were and what they thought of us—you're a dyke, he's a queer, blood tells, and your whole family's fucked up.

And he said it with my mama standing right there.

"Beau's never played outside alone," I told him again, 'cause I needed that bastard to find my baby brother, so there was no use in calling him out. It'd only upset Mama.

"Well, he probably wandered down the driveway to the road," the sheriff said. "I'll get my boys to search around. When'd he leave?"

Davis stared off into the swamp. I think he knew then. "Mama went to the store 'round one o'clock," he told us. "She came back about two, and we been looking since then."

"I didn't ask that," Sheriff Irwin said. "I asked when he left."

"I dunno when he left. I was upstairs working." Davis crossed his arms tighter. "It could've been any time. He could've left right after she did, or he could've left five minutes before she came home. But I told him to stay downstairs and to nod if he would, and he nodded."

"Then why isn't he inside?" I asked. "Beau wouldn't say he'd stay downstairs then walk out the door."

"Well, he did." Davis wore that mean, cornered look, pursed up and drawn in. "And he didn't say a damn word, he just nodded, so don't you make it sound to the sheriff like he talked."

"I didn't say he talked," I told Davis. "Beau doesn't talk, but that doesn't mean you can't understand him."

The sheriff asked more questions, like what was Beau wearing and did he have shoes on and did we have a recent picture of him. Mama couldn't answer, so when he asked all that stuff he looked at me, 'cause who else would they expect dressed him and kept track of his shoes? Quentin did as much as me, but of course they wouldn't think that. If Mama couldn't take care of Beau, they figured I did it.

Mama said she had to make coffee for the deputies and went inside. But mostly she needed something to do while they drove around. She couldn't stand in the driveway and wait while she worried about her baby.

Davis went in with her. "I don't think we should leave Mama alone," he told us. But he didn't want to face us asking questions. We knew he was a liar. With people going inside, I hoped Quentin and I had cleaned the kitchen that morning. I didn't remember. Of course, Quentin cleaned as much as I did, but in the end it'd fall on Mama and me if they went in and found a mess. They'd say, Why did she let the kitchen get in this state? Doesn't Lila help her? And it would be one more thing to add up against us.

They thought Mama was lazy 'cause Quentin and I sat out cotillion, and they thought she was lazy 'cause I didn't do pageants or at least riding lessons. Then when I was fourteen I cut my hair short—no shorter than it is now, but down there they worship long-haired blondes. If you're under twenty-five and you got hair on your head you grow it out, and if the Lord God gave you the misfortune of brown hair, well, a lotta things can take care of that. Mama had her hair highlighted—and by highlighted I mean almost all-the-way-dyed—once a month. So when I cut mine off people talked.

"Why'd you cut off that hair, Caroline Candice?" Miz Brewster asked me. She owned Brewster's Diner and whatever I said would get passed around Lower Congaree like a bad cold. "You had just the prettiest long hair."

"It was hot," I told her. "It kept getting in my face."

"Huh," she said, and that was all. But she had a sour-lemon look when she said it, like I'd done something wrong and maybe dangerous. People said a lot more than that about it, things about Mama and things about me. I didn't understand a lot then. Like I didn't understand that I didn't have a chest, so why did I need a bra? And Mama didn't tell me to wear one. When I was fourteen I was flat as Quentin. He finally had to say it.

"Why don't you wear a bra?" he asked, and he was blushing.
"I don't need one. Obviously." I huffed 'cause why was he making me admit I was flat as a damn pancake? I didn't really care but I did, sort of.

"Um, you kinda do need one." Quentin was kicking at the grass and crossing his arms.

"Quentin, I look in the mirror every damn day. I know I don't have boobs and you don't have to act like I do to make me feel better or something."

He focused on that grass at our feet, not my face. "I'm not talking about your actual boobs, Lila. Your, uh—goddammit. You know when you get cold?"

"What are you talking about?" I asked.

I still didn't get it. That's how dense I was.

"Fuck. I can see your nipples, okay? You didn't have to make me say it." He was close to crying. "The other guys were talking about it. They said you didn't have any tits but they loved looking anyway. That's how they are. They're like that about you 'cause you're pretty and I hate it. You didn't have to make me say it, Lila. Get Mama to buy you some decent bras. I hate hearing them talk about you."

Quentin ran away. I think he was crying by the end of it. I wanted to cry. I wanted to cry while we were standing in that driveway too, but I couldn't. If I cried they'd say, Poor Lila, I know it's so hard, why don't you go help your mama and take your mind off things? But if I didn't cry, they'd think, Why isn't she crying? Her baby brother goes missing, and she stands there like she doesn't give a rat's ass. God, what a bitch. She let her mama go off into the kitchen with that Davis to help, and you know he's no goddamn help at all. You see how she got raised? Blood tells.

I had to pick if I wanted to be poor Lila or if I wanted to be a bitch, and I wouldn't leave Quentin alone. I hated him then, but I still loved him, too. So I picked bitch. They muttered behind their hands at me, but they didn't say it out loud. That was something at least.

It was Columbus Day, the middle of October, and my tank top stuck to my back. Mama's garden thermometer hit ninety while we stewed in that rotten swamp-smell. Quentin and I watched the treeline, all those bald cypresses standing like guard towers and the dimmed nothing beyond. If I prayed at all, I'd've prayed Beau was safe back there, but I stopped praying when Daddy died.

Whenever one of the deputies passed, he eyed me up slow, like it didn't matter who saw. I felt those stares like bugs crawling. They didn't try to hide it.

"I wish they wouldn't do that," I said to Quentin.

"Do what?" he asked.

"Look at me like that."

He cut his eyes over. "Then why're you wearing that shirt?"

I had on a black tank top. It violated school dress code—I was showing my shoulders—but mostly, it looked like Sarah Connor's shirt at the end of *Terminator 2*, just untucked. Maybe it came down a little farther. God, I loved that shirt. I had three identical ones and I wore them all the time, partly 'cause I liked them, and partly 'cause I liked Sarah Connor.

"It shouldn't matter what shirt I wear," I told Quentin.

"Lila," Quentin whispered. "It's cut low and your bra pushes your tits together. When you dress like that I can't stop them from hurting you."

I pulled my arms tight against me and felt sorta sick. That shirt wasn't cut low and I hated Quentin saying it more than I hated those men staring.

"I'm just telling you the truth," he said. "I don't wanna be mean." Quentin believed every word and every word hurt him. "I don't like them looking either. I hate when they look at you. They only want one thing."

"You know all about that," I told him. By then those long cypress-shadows had crept over us.

"Lila." He touched my arm and I pushed him off. "I should've never—"

"No, you shouldn't've," I told him. "And I said don't talk about it again and I meant don't talk about it again."

We stood a little apart in the drive after that and I hated it, 'cause I loved Quentin even if I hated him too, but at least he was something in the middle of that misery. I kept my arms crossed. The men still stared at me.

Sheriff Irwin talked on his radio. At first I jumped every time it crackled, and I hoped someone would say, We found him, we're bringing him home, but I learned fast that those radios were only grown-up toys. The shadows stretched longer and dusk dropped down, sunset one moment, then graying twilight an eyeblink later. It happened like that around October in Lower Congaree. Night would swallow a day whole. When that gray came, I stepped up to the sheriff.

"I think you need to look in the swamp," I said. "You looked on the roads long enough. Beau might've gone off into the swamp."

Quentin could've backed me up, but he stayed quiet.

The sheriff hated anyone getting in his business. I was a teenage girl—a teenage girl with short hair in a Sarah Connor black tank top. We might've had money but our father was dead, and our mother couldn't keep up the place. We were one of the oldest families in town, but that didn't matter anymore; our family silver didn't matter anymore 'cause they said that blood tells, blood will always tell.

The sheriff spit tobacco at my feet. "It's too late to go in the swamp," he said. "There's gators and snakes and back there, and you can't hardly see your hand in front of your face. If your brother's back in there he ain't moving til morning."

"You don't know that, I told him. "How d'you know what Beau would do?"

He squinted at me. Night was falling fast. "I know what I'll tell my men to do, and I'm not telling them to go out in that swamp."

"You scared of what's out there?" I asked.

The sheriff popped his jaw. "I got no idea what you're talking about."

"You do so."

The sheriff had been annoyed, but in that gathering dark, he went over into something altogether different, something bleak and flinted and iron-hard, and he took a moment before he spoke again. "You oughta be in the kitchen with your mama."

"You oughta be in that swamp looking for my brother," I told him.

He'd've hit me if he could. He'd've backhanded me right across the mouth. But even if we didn't have a father there were things he couldn't do. "We'll keep searching the roads tonight," he said.

"We're gonna use your house as a base of operations, and we're gonna search the roads and the rest of the property in case he shows up. You get on inside, Caroline Candice. Quentin, you take her inside, you hear me?"

"C'mon, Lila." Quentin picked up my hand. I pulled away. Sheriff Irwin expected me to say yessir and follow Quentin into the kitchen. That's how it worked there. I was a girl and this was men's business and I oughta be in the kitchen helping my mama.

"You need to look in the swamp," I told him instead. "My baby brother's in that swamp and he's scared." I grit my teeth and balled my fists, 'cause I couldn't think about how Beau had to sleep with the light on, not then.

"You think I don't know how to do my job, little girl?" When he said it, he looked right down my tank top.

"I think you don't know how to find my brother." I started to shake then, and if he noticed he'd laugh. If he laughed, his deputies would laugh, and they'd all tell me where I oughta be.

"You think you could do better? You might know 'bout finding boys, but you don't know 'bout that swamp." The sheriff's mouth twisted into a smirk. "Or maybe you don't know nothing 'bout finding boys, Caroline Candice."

One of the deputies, Garth Baxter, snorted laughter. "She don't have to find boys," he said. "She has to beat them off with a stick."

"Beat them off is right," said Ed Hines. "I got something she can beat off." He said it quiet, but he said it.

"Fuck off," I told him. "Get in that swamp and find my little brother, you sick bastard. How old're you? I just turned eighteen and you're what, thirty-five?"

"Oh, you're legal now," he said. "That makes things easier."

"Go to hell." Quentin's eyes narrowed in that near-dark and he looked mean as Davis then. "Don't you say that shit about my sister."

Ed barely spared a glance for Quentin. "You try and stop me."

They never would've said it if I had a daddy or my mama could keep up the place. They wouldn't've dared. But we were Carsons, and that made us fair game.

"You feel like a big man with that gun?" Quentin asked. "Does it compensate?"

Ed wrinkled his nose. "What the hell are you talking about?"

"Quentin, shut up," I told him. "Just shut up."

"No, they're gonna stop talking about you like that," he said. "They're gonna stop looking down your shirt and treat you like they treat their own sisters."

"What, like fucking them?" I asked.

Those men thought I was calling them redneck bastards, and normally they'd hit someone for a crack like that, but you couldn't hit a girl. But Quentin knew what I meant, and he knew I meant it for him. He couldn't say anything with those deputies there, and he probably hated me more for it.

"You get your little ass in that kitchen," said one of the deputies from the shadows. "And you best go real quick before your mouth runs quicker than your brother can."

"You never answered my question," Sheriff Irwin said to me. "You tell me if you think you can do better."

"I think you should do your damn job," I told him.

He didn't drop his eyes and I wouldn't drop mine. "You ever been back in that swamp?" he asked. "I been back there, and I seen things. Don't you tell me to take my men there at night. You got no idea. I wouldn't send my men back there for my own mother right now."

He spit at my feet again.

"You can take that to the head of South Carolina Law Enforcement. I'll stand in front of Judge Lanier down at the county courthouse and say the same thing to him I'm saying to you right now.

I won't send my deputies back there at night, you hear me? Quentin's gonna take you inside now, and you tell your mama we're still searching the roads."

When he brought in the district judge I knew I'd lost.

It'd keep getting worse for me after that. I could say yessir, sorry sir, and leave with some kinda pride. Or I could keep fighting, and those deputies would keep making nasty side comments, and sooner or later, if Quentin didn't punch someone, he'd have to say something bad enough to make them punch him first. They'd beat him half-dead and claim in court he attacked them, but he'd have to do it. That's how it worked. He couldn't stand there while they talked about his sister that way.

"Yessir," I said. "Sorry sir."

Sheriff Irwin rested a hand on my shoulder and looked right down my shirt again. "You're worried about your little brother, honey," he told me. "We understand. Go make sure your mama's okay, now."

Quentin and I went into the house.

Chapter Four

Lila spoke as if she were talking to herself rather than another person. Had she ever told her story before? Her voice seemed dreamy and faraway; her eyes stayed unfocused, as if something other than crumbled popcorning loomed above her.

"Your brother," I said. "Beau. Did he have autism?"

Lila blinked a few times, like she had forgotten about me and found my presence a mild surprise. "I don't know," she replied. "I mean, probably. But I don't know."

I searched her face, still so distant and distracted. "What do you mean, you don't know? The doctors couldn't decide?"

She seemed to snap back to me and turned on her side. Her pretty dark hair fell in her face. "No, I mean I don't know."

I came up with nothing and so simply stared.

"It's—it's unforgivable. I understand that." She hesitated. "But that's how it worked down there. Mama took Beau to doctors when he didn't talk, but I think when they said something big was wrong, she stopped."

"But there could have been therapies for him."

"Of course, Mama and Daddy understood something was wrong." She chewed her lip for a moment, as if she were searching for words. "It's not like they thought he was like everyone else. The doctors could've said, 'Your son has severe autism, he'll never speak or live on his own,' and she couldn't deal with it, so she decided not to deal with it at all."

What could I hand her in the face of that madness? "So you have no idea if your brother had brain damage, or autism, or another, possibly treatable, condition?"

Lila pushed herself up on an elbow. "There was something wrong with him, and that was all. It didn't matter what you called it. You don't understand how it is down there, McKenzie." She settled back onto her pillows. "To them, trying to make Beau do more would've been undignified. You might as well tell a person in a wheelchair to stand up and walk."

I could only blink at her.

"That's how it works. That's what I'm trying to tell you." Impatience slipped into her voice. "Do you want to hear it?"

"Yes," I said.

Lila began again.

CHAPTER FIVE

2016

When we walked into the mudroom, Quentin kicked off his fake Rainbows. I didn't notice anyone until Mike Harner said, "Nice shoes, Carson. Your mama buy those for you at Hopkins?"

Mike was one of the cool kids in our class at Congaree High, and his daddy was Sheriff Irwin's head deputy. He'd tagged along, like Beau gone missing made some interesting field trip.

"Yeah, these sandals came from Hopkins. Why the hell d'you care?" Quentin asked. He should've ignored Mike. But he was mad the men wouldn't look for Beau, and he was mad the men had started in on me, and he was mad about what I'd said. It was hard to say which he was madder about, but he was mad, and he wanted to fight. If he couldn't fight the sheriff, he'd fight something else. Quentin had a long, long fuse, but when he reached the end he was worse than Davis.

"Quentin," I said. "C'mon."

"You can afford real Rainbows," Mike told him. "You're too fucking lazy to drive into Columbia for 'em."

"Maybe I don't wanna spend the money."

Mike looked at Quentin like he might look at gum stuck to pavement. "Maybe your daddy was okay, but y'all are fucking useless. Your mama's roof ain't nailed tight, and the rest of y'all sit around on your lazy asses and read books." He paused, and a sick smirk crept up his cheeks. "I bet you write poetry, don't you, Quentin?"

Quentin shoved Mike hard enough that his head hit the white-washed wall. "Keep your fucking mouth shut," he said, and Mike went wide-eyed and open-mouthed as a startled bullfrog. "Y'hear me? Keep my family outta your goddamn mouth."

"Quentin, stop it," I told him. "Mama's gonna hear and it's bad enough already."

"No." Quentin shoved Mike again. "He's gonna apologize and he's gonna shut his mouth."

Night had dropped down, black and full of high, cold stars. Mama's fretting rose from the kitchen. "My baby's alone in the dark," she was saying. "He might be cold. What if my baby's cold?"

"You Carsons been going downhill since your father died," Mike told him, and he looked Quentin in the eye when he said it. "Everybody knows it. Now you lost your little brother? Who the fuck loses a kid?"

For a blistering, drawn-out moment, nothing happened, and the world seemed to hang there, Mike's face twisting, Quentin frozen in rage. I opened my mouth to say Quentin, don't. Don't you do it. But before I could speak, Mike's nose crunched wetly under my brother's fist. The deputy's son grabbed his face and howled like a baby while blood dripped between his fingers.

"Oh dammit, Q, you did it now," I said. "They're gonna kill your ass."

Davis banged into the mudroom, glanced at Mike, closed his eyes, and swore very quietly. "Quentin, did you have to?" he asked. "Did you really really have to?"

Quentin shook out his hand.

Deputies roared through the back door. Someone threw my twin face-first against our own damn wall. His neck wrenched sideways and his cheek slammed the plaster and Davis yanked me back. I kicked Davis and started yelling that Mike had started it, Mike had talked about us, and Quentin practically had to hit him. Quentin shouted. Davis started up in that stupid reasonable voice like he could talk those men outta something when we didn't have a father. Mike was a deputy's kid, and Quentin had been fighting with the sheriff. They didn't care who said what. Mike had a broken nose, and Quentin had bloody knuckles.

They threw him into cuffs right in our mudroom. "I'm sorry, I'm so sorry," Quentin kept saying. "I shouldn't've done it."

They hauled him out the door and Mama's voice rose behind us. "Lila," she was calling. "Lila, what's going on? Where're they taking him? What's going on? Lila? Quentin?"

I ran out behind them. No one seemed to notice. They dragged Quentin back to the sheriff and threw him again. His knees hit the ground and he folded in half, but thank God he kept his balance. With his hands cuffed behind, he'd've hit face-first and broke his own nose on the driveway. They'd probably hoped for that.

"What the hell is this?" the sheriff roared. Blue light made the cops seem sharp-edged and hungry. That blue drew the cypresses darker and closer, like a looming promise I'd never imagined and didn't want to.

"He broke the Harner boy's nose just now," said Bam-Bam McAllister. They had the stupidest nicknames.

"What, did you think you'd hit him instead of me?" Sheriff Irwin asked.

Quentin didn't answer. He was still barefoot.

The sheriff toed his knee, hard. "Answer me. D'you hit the Harner boy?"

If he didn't start talking, they'd start punching. I knew it, and I guess Quentin knew it, too. I hugged myself. They were so busy watching him that they hadn't seen me in the shadows.

"Yessir," Quentin said. "I hit him."

"You tell me why you thought that was a goddamn good idea," Sheriff Irwin said. "I could take you down to Legare County lockup and hold you for twenty-four hours without charging you."

"He talked about my family," Quentin told him. "Sir."

The sheriff spit, and he didn't hit Quentin, but he came close. "He talked about your family?"

"Yessir. I told him to keep my family outta his mouth."

"What, that boy said you Carsons can't keep your shit together? Is that what he said?" the sheriff asked. "You don't have a daddy so you need me to tell you. When someone says that shit and you punch them in the face, you make it true."

I hated that sheriff. I hated all of them.

"He asked me who the fuck loses a kid," Quentin said.

The sheriff poked Quentin's leg with his toe. "Apparently you Carsons do."

Quentin couldn't argue 'cause it was true. Davis never should've let Beau walk out that door. He ditched my little brother so he could finish his accounting work. He probably said, Go downstairs and play while I finish this work, Beau. I bet Davis never even thought to tell him, Don't go outside. Or if he did, he said it like he didn't care, and Beau went outside anyway.

Davis didn't care, and that was the truth of it. Beau didn't matter. Davis was the heir and Quentin was the spare and I was for Mama, but Beau didn't count. He'd gone off into the swamp 'cause he didn't count. He'd finally realized it that summer—Mama saying he was born wrong, then making him sleep by himself. Us dragging him places then finally not taking him anywhere at all. Beau knew.

So when the sheriff told Quentin we lost kids neither of us couldn't say anything. I grit my teeth and forced myself not to cry. If I cried they'd find me.

"Your mama can't keep this house together," Sheriff Irwin said. "Half them shutters need nailed up and you got shingles missing on that roof. Those trees need trimmed back 'fore they take out your power lines. Gutters need cleaned out. They been clogged up so long you got plants growing in 'em. That swamp's 'bout eating your house."

He was right about that, too.

"You boys could do it," he told Quentin. "You boys could get up there and do it but you don't."

"I— don't know how," Quentin said.

And even if he did know how he didn't have time. We didn't have time for things like that.

"'Course you don't know how to clean a gutter. It's not in one of your books."

Quentin kept his head down. There wasn't anything to say.

I could've told Mama to call people. I could've said, Mama, call someone to clean the gutters. But she wouldn't't've known who to call or what to say on the phone, 'cause Mama hated talking on the phone. It would've ended with her crying 'cause she couldn't keep up the house. Then I would've had to tell Davis, Call a man to clean out the gutters, and we'd've ended up in a fight about it. Who the hell has money to get the gutters cleaned out when Mama stopped growing tobacco and won't even keep up the hay fields? Davis would ask. You got money to get the gutters cleaned out, Lila? Oh, you don't? Then shut up about it or get your ass up there and do it yourself.

But I didn't have time to do it any more than Quentin did.

"I guess you finally did get your nose out of those books and do something for once," the sheriff said. He grabbed my twin's arm and hauled him up. "You're gonna sit tonight out."

"What?" Quentin asked.

"You throw a sir on the end of that." The sheriff popped open his cruiser and my chest hurt. "Get in there, and I best not hear a peep 'less you gotta piss. Then you bang on the window and one of the deputies'll get you."

"How am I supposed to bang on the window if I'm cuffed?" Quentin asked.

"You get creative, and I told you to throw a sir on the end of that or I'll make you wish you did." Sheriff Irwin chucked Quentin in the back like you might throw a gym bag, then slammed the door shut.

"Well, that took care of that," the sheriff said. "Now we just gotta deal with his smart-mouth dyke sister."

I stayed very still in those shadows.

"I got something to shut her mouth," Mike's daddy told them. At first, I thought he meant his fist, but he grabbed his crotch and they all laughed.

"Not if I can shut it first," said Jack Richardson, and their laughter rose again. His son John-John had gone to school with me for thirteen years, same as Mike Harner. Those deputies had seen me graduate from kindergarten. We'd worn tiny mortarboards and sung "The Alphabet Song," then "The Itsy-Bitsy Spider."

Garth Baxter lit a cigarette. He was only a few years older than me. "Why d'you even want it?" he asked, and his orange cherry flared when he breathed in. "Bet her brothers had it first. You know how it goes with these people."

I couldn't breathe. If I choked, they'd hear me.

"Fuck that," Ed Hines said. "Maybe Davis did, but that one in the car's a damn queer, and she's a little dyke like he just said. They'd just sit in a room staring at each other."

"Bet you I could change her mind." Bam-Bam snagged one of Garth's cigarettes, and when he flicked the lighter, his face lit up eerie and vicious.

I hadn't come out. I never came out in Lower Congaree. I was a skinny girl with shortish hair who wore Doc Martens and listened to Green Day, the Sex Pistols if I felt 'specially dangerous that day. We didn't have a Hot Topic—Columbiana Mall was fifty minutes and a world away. Sometimes I Sharpied my nails black, but that's all. Think pink Pale Waves shirts and black beanies and some gloves I chopped the fingers off. No piercings. No tats. Those Doc Martens were standard-issue, plain-ass Docs I wore with regular old dark jeans. I'd've been laughed out of a punk show.

And I wasn't all or nothing. I liked Trent Reznor before he bulked out and Billy Joe from Green Day—the skinny, guyliner types. I never said I liked girls. Never to anyone but Quentin, and I only told him sideways. Those men had guessed, and it terrified me. Quentin had been right the year before. We'd been driving home from school; the leaves were going tired green from September's heat and the windows were down.

"We never been to a school dance," I said. "We should go to homecoming."

Quentin glanced away from the road and stared as if I'd suggested we drown ourselves.

"No, Lila," he said. "You can't."

"Why not?" I asked. "Mama could watch Beau for one damn night. It's only one night."

He shook his head once, but hard and decisive. "You can't. You know what they want to do to you. You're beautiful. They'll hurt you if you go to a dance. Don't you understand that?"

"It's not like I'd do anything with the guy. I mean I wouldn't want to." I smiled a little. I came close to it. I said it and I didn't say it.

Quentin shook his head harder and I worried he would drive off the road. "Don't Lila. You can't go with a guy and you can't say things like that, either."

"Why the hell not?" I slumped back in the seat, angry.

"Those guys only want one thing," he told me. "They'll hurt you to get it. I'm a guy and I know."

"But I meant—" I started, and I was about to say it.

"No." Quentin held up a hand. "Uh-uh. No, Lila. You can't and we won't talk about it anymore."

That was the first crack. That, right there. Quentin and I had never said we wouldn't talk about something before. We talked about everything. Who else was there to talk to? Our father was dead, our mother wasn't all there, and Davis was busy being Davis-the-heir. Perfect Davis, Davis who people clucked over. With everything gone to ruin, they'd say, he was trying to hold the whole world together. Who do you think does his goddamn laundry, I always wanted to yell. You think you can hold the world together without someone to wash your dirty underwear, then you're sadly mistaken.

The darkness around our broken-shuttered house kept me safe. I wanted to go inside with Mama, but I had to wait until no one was watching, and that took a long time. The men paced and Sheriff Irwin talked on his radio. Beau was in the swamp. God only knew what could happen out there under those dark cypress shadows. No one was gonna find him. If he'd've been alone I could've lived with it. But whatever was out there had him, that thing that watched and waited, and that was the worst part.

He liked to be alone—Beau could play by himself for hours—but when night came he wanted one of us. That summer Mama had decided he had to learn to sleep by himself. Usually he slept with me or Quentin or Mama, but that night she told him good night, shut his bedroom door, and stood in front of it.

He cried and kicked the door. "You get in your bed and go to sleep," Mama told him. "You gotta learn to sleep by yourself."

Beau sobbed. She'd left him in the dark, too.

I begged her to stop. "He can sleep in my room," I said. "You can put a bed in there for him."

"No," she told me. "He has to learn to sleep alone."

"Mama, he doesn't want to. He doesn't need to say the word no for you to figure that out." I was almost crying myself 'cause Beau's crying and kicking had gone down to whimpers. That whimpering meant he'd given up, and it was the worst sound.

"He'll calm down," Mama said. "He needs to learn."

I wanted to ask, Why is it so important to teach him to sleep alone when you don't teach him how to tie his shoes? If it's so important to teach him to sleep by himself, why don't you teach him to do other things for himself too? But she didn't mind tying his shoes or picking out his clothes. She minded dealing with him at night, so Beau had to sleep by himself.

Mama never went into my room, so the next day, I dragged a cot from the attic and set it up on the far side of my bed. That night, Mama did it again. She shut Beau's door, and she had to hold it there 'cause he beat on it while he cried. "You wait and he'll quiet down," she told me.

"You're too soft on him, Lila."

"I don't understand why," I said.

"Well, you won't always be here to baby him," she said.

I had to wait. It took Beau a long time to stop. I waited in my room 'cause I couldn't stand to listen to his sad little whimpering. When Mama finally left I crept down the hall and opened his door slow so it didn't creak. Beau was sitting up in bed with his cartoon pajamas on and his quilt wrapped around and around himself.

"Do you wanna sleep here, or do you want to sleep in a special bed in my room?" I asked.

He tore his quilt off and ran to me.

"You have to be a sneaky sneaker," I said. "You have to be very, very quiet like a mouse so no one hears."

He followed me down the hall. After that, Beau slept in his little cot in my room. Sometimes I did homework while he fell asleep, and sometimes I went to sleep, too. He didn't wanna be alone, and what was so bad about that?

"Beau sleeps in your room, doesn't he?" Quentin asked one afternoon when Mama had gone out.

I didn't answer.

"You'll spoil him," he said. "He needs to learn to sleep by himself. What's he gonna do when we go to college?" I turned a page like I hadn't heard him talking. He didn't exist in my world at that particular moment.

"You don't wanna be alone in your room," Quentin said.

My lungs buckled inward like something had stolen all my air, but I focused on the words in front of me. They'd make sense if I could read them.

"You want Beau there so no one will come in," Quentin told me.

I forced a hard breath. "Stop it. I ask him if he wants to come in 'cause he's the one who's scared."

He drew inward like he was waiting to get hit. "I was trying to say you didn't have to."

"I said don't talk about it," I snapped.

"And I was saying you didn't need to be scared." Quentin drew his arms close despite the pounding heat. "I didn't—"

"Just don't."

He walked away, and I choked on my own stupid tears. Did I want to cry 'cause I was scared or 'cause he left? I understand now it was both.

Quentin was on the far side of the cruiser with his head resting against its window. Right about then, I should've been sneaking in to get Beau. I should've been leading him down the hall and tucking him into his army cot. Goodnight, Beau, I should've been whispering. Instead he was gone and Quentin was in police custody. Maybe he belonged there. I dropped my head as those cars threw their awful lights over my house, over those broken shutters and missing shingles and clogged-up gutters. More ways the Carsons failed. The deputies looked at those shutters like they'd've looked at my little brother. My throat caught, and without anyone to see, I took a long, shuddery breath and cried without a sound. I cried for a long time.

Sheriff Irwin had Quentin cuffed and locked in that cruiser 'cause our father was dead and it didn't matter. I waited for the men to look away. Those bastards weren't searching for Beau, not really. They were joyriding down Legare County's back roads.

I tried not to look, but that black swamp kept drawing me in. Blue lights threw it into shadows that shifted and danced like cold fire. Beau was lost out there, and God knew what was out there with him. The longer I looked the more I felt it. The hairs on my neck rose—you know that feeling, when you're sure if you whirl around you'll catch someone staring. I hated it then, and that ancient thing hated me back.

It is ancient, too. Whatever's back there, it's always been there. Dale Brewster told me he's seen deer stop sweaty and trembling at those cypresses. They snort and roll their eye-whites, but they'd rather face a pack of hunting dogs than go farther. Every hunter knows phone batteries don't last in that swamp—and keep in mind they don't go far back, not into the deep part. Before phones, everyone would bitch that their GPS could never find a satellite. Compasses spin. I've seen that happen, and it'll stop you dead, just staring at it. People take a ten-minute shortcut they've known their whole lives, and when they reach the end, an hour's passed.

These things happen in that swamp. You stand on the edge of those trees and smell that sweet-rot. You wait. You'll feel it watching you, and you'll know. Beau must've felt it watching. But maybe it wasn't the same for him. Maybe it didn't watch him. Maybe it called instead.

The moon was a high, round eye. It dipped low behind the trees, as if they'd reached up to snatch it. The men paced and talked. No one slept, and people moved through the kitchen.

Eventually some deputies went inside, and Quentin kicked at the door until the other two dragged him out. "I gotta pee," he said. Sheriff Irwin was on his radio and while no one was looking, I ran inside. The door slammed behind me, and then they all knew where I'd been. But at least I was safe.

Mama looked up from the table. Her eyes were red and her nose was red and she slumped on her elbows. "Nice of you to show up, Caroline Candice," she said. "Real kind of you to let us wonder where the hell you were on top of—"

She choked up and couldn't say any more.

Davis had that tight line of a mouth, that big-brother, you're the man of the house now face. "We were worried," he said. "The deputies swore they hadn't seen you."

"They hadn't," I told him. "I followed Q out and I hid until they weren't looking."

"Uh-huh." He kept that mean, tight look. "Yeah, Lila."

I didn't understand. With everything happening—with Beau missing, with Quentin locked in that police car—it took some time. When it dawned on me I felt sick.

"It wasn't like that," I said.

I could've thrown up right there in our kitchen. I saw it happening, saw vomit splattering and sticking in the cracks between the hardwoods while all those deputies watched and laughed behind their hands. Davis thought: Beau's lost in the swamp, Quentin got his dumbass thrown in a police car, and Lila's out back fucking around with one of those goddamn deputies.

"I'm going to bed," Mama said. She pushed back her chair and unfolded like an old woman. "I can't stay up and watch this. Imma take a pill and y'all wake me when they go out to look for my baby in the morning."

"Do you want me—" I started to say.

"No Caroline Candice," she practically snapped. "I don't."

Then it was my turn to sag down, and she stomped over those cypress hardwoods, that floor hewn from the swamp I couldn't escape, not even in my own house. No one spoke as she banged through the rooms, then up the stairs. When she'd gone, a hand closed over my arm. I was too tired to fight Davis as he dragged me through the dining room and the sunroom and onto the side porch. The door rattled when he slammed it.

"Who was it?" he asked, and he held me so tight he'd leave marks. "You tell me which one of 'em it was."

"No one," I said. "I told you, I was watching Quentin."

"Liar."

I whipped my head up. "You're the liar. You didn't tell Beau to stay inside, and if you did you said it like you didn't care, and he didn't nod."

Our side porch wasn't glassed-in but screened, and I could smell that swamp, all murky, summer fermented scum. Davis yanked me hard. "I can't believe Mama raised such a slut," he said. "I don't know who all's out there but one of 'em had you behind the house or in the barn. Why else would you be gone so long?"

"I told you—"

Davis dragged his fingers through my hair. I yanked away, but his grip only tightened. "No hay. They didn't have you in the main

50

barn. Either you were on your knees or in a tobacco shed or on the ground outside."

"You sick fuck." I was close to crying but I got in his face anyway. "D'you get off on thinking about your little sister—"

He let go of my arm and slapped me across the mouth.

I took three slow steps back and touched my face. I remember every step. I remember picking up each foot, and shifting it back, and that rug rucking up under them. I remember my own slow breath and my heart betraying me when it drummed faster. I raised my hand and I touched my face. He hadn't hit me hard enough to bruise, but he'd hit me hard enough. How hard is hard enough, I wondered. Does that mean hard enough to make me quiet, or hard enough to scare me, or hard enough to teach me a lesson, and if it's hard enough to teach me a lesson, is that lesson about being a slut, or calling him names?

"Don't you dare," Davis told me. "You caused enough trouble tonight. Did you see Mama? You should've been in here helping her."

"I was—"

"I heard enough of you lying. Keep your mouth shut. I bet you're too dumb to use protection, you fucking hick. That's all y'all are, you know that?" he said. "Daddy's dead and Mama's crazy and y'all just sit on your asses up here. Least I try."

I held my face. He hadn't bothered to turn on a light. Blue flashed like rhythmic lightning and made Davis seem sculpted as the statue of an angry god.

He laughed short and bitter. "Barefoot and pregnant, that's what you're gonna end up. You'll be lucky if you know who the daddy is. You oughta hope Quentin has the balls to make someone speak up and say it's theirs, 'cause I ain't getting involved."

I took another step back.

"Maybe Quentin should just shut them all up and say it's his. Show them what fucking hicks y'all really are."

He might as well have hit me again. Davis would keep at me until he was done, and I didn't need slapped across the mouth again to figure that out. Dark blazed into sudden, startling blue as he lectured me. I was a slut and a whore. We'd ruined our family, me and Quentin and Beau and Mama, ruined it for good after he and Daddy had done everything, and we might as well not be Carsons, but Burrs like Mama. Our bad blood came down from her side, and we ruined the Carson name.

He said I was the worst, and Mama ought've raised me right. I never should've run around with Quentin and worn his clothes. I was pretty and could've made something of myself. Instead I was out back with one of those sheriff's deputies like any trailer trash. "Nothing wrong with you being smart," Davis said. "But you're gonna be barefoot and pregnant in nine months like every other redneck skank in this town."

He went on and on until I only heard a word here and there. Slut. Stupid-ass. Lazy. Quentin called me perfect. He wanted me to stay that way and he would keep me like a princess in a tower if he could have me. Davis said I was a whore and I'd never convince him otherwise.

Mama thought I'd been with one of those men, too. He'd told her so, and she believed him, 'cause he was Davis and he was right.

I took it. I waited for it to end as that blue rolled on and off, on and off like waves crashing in through the sticky-sweet smell of that swamp, and it took a long time. Beau was alone with whatever watched and waited out there. Mama was asleep, or trying to be. Quentin was locked in a police car. Davis wouldn't stop calling me names. I just hoped everyone in that kitchen couldn't hear.

He finally walked out and left me alone. I could've gone back to the kitchen, but I went up to my room instead. I couldn't do it anymore. I was a Madonna or the Whore of Babylon, and I always would be. All the time Beau was small and cold and caught by whatever watched and waited in that swamp. Mama had an heir and a spare. She didn't need anything else, and I wouldn't be something for someone else. I wouldn't have men shaking their heads and saying blood will tell, or grabbing their dicks and saying they had something to shut my mouth with. Fuck the broken shutters and the closed fourth floor.

I curled in my bed and sobbed.

Then I changed into thick cargo pants, boots, and a long-sleeved shirt I hoped would keep off bugs. Mosquitoes would swarm—there would always be mosquitoes—but chiggers left itchy welts, and blackflies bit til blood ran. They'd all drink Deet like Kool-Aid, and better to be hot in a long-sleeved shirt than go mad from their slow vampirism. In the attic I found an old hiking pack from Davis's days in Boy Scouts, one of those with a water bladder snaking out of it, so I cleaned that and filled it. I threw in a flashlight, then two packs of matches and a lighter. I'd be lost when I needed them, and I'd want the light. Once I had that pack together, I left it next to Beau's little cot and walked down to the kitchen.

The hardwoods had been clean at least, but those men had tracked mud behind them. They weren't even decent enough to wipe their feet. I ignored them slouching around our table and made myself a cup of coffee. Davis wasn't there, and maybe he'd gone to bed.

"Make me one of those while you're up, honey," said Ed Hines. "We got a long day ahead of us."

He was going out to look for Beau, and even if he wasn't I couldn't be a bitch in my own kitchen. You've gotta understand that: those men were sitting in my kitchen. Satan could've parked himself at that table and I'd've offered him sweet tea. If he'd've stayed longer than ten minutes I'd've fed him.

I poured another cup of coffee. "You want cream or sugar?" I asked.

"Black as my soul, baby girl," he said, and they laughed.

"I'll take a cup if you don't mind, Lila," Garth told me. "Black too, please."

Then I had to get them all coffee, or warm up the cups they had. Every one of 'em smiled, and every one of 'em said thank you.

Bam-Bam banged in. He didn't wipe his feet, either. "Kid's still in the patrol car," he told them. "I had to uncuff him to take a piss, but I cuffed him back up again."

A few of them snorted a kind of quick laugh.

"Useless bastard," Bam-Bam said. "He could hardly hold his own dick."

They laughed louder. "Cuffs're a bitch," Jack Richardson said. "Lucky you didn't need to hold it for him, Bam-Bam."

Bam-Bam glared. "I'd've let him piss his pants before I held his dick."

"You know we're just messing around, honey," Jack told me. Thirteen years I'd gone to school with his son. He'd seen me graduate from kindergarten, and he'd made jokes about fucking me the night before. That's what I was to them. "You know how men get," he said. "Warm up my coffee for me?"

I poured more coffee in his cup and set more on to brew.

"You're not like your brothers, Lila," Mike Harner's daddy told me. "It's a sad thing, you up in this house like this."

The men were quiet for a moment. "Damn shame," Garth said finally. "It's a damn shame."

"It's not—" I started.

"Oh, baby girl, you don't have to pretend," Jack told me.

"I'm not pretending," I said as I focused on those hardwoods. At least I had plenty of clothes on.

"You're too pretty to stay up here. I bet you get worked to the bone with your mama the way she is. You take care of that little brother of yours, don't you?" Jack asked.

"Well sometimes," I said. "But he likes me best."

"'Course he does." Jack sounded kind and I hated him for it. "He likes you best 'cause you take care of him so well. You take care of everything up here, don't you, Lila?"

Quentin and I both worked our asses off to keep that house together and keep Beau happy and keep Mama from crying about this, that, or the other. Davis didn't see it, but that bastard Jack did, and I hated them both for it. Of course I teared up, 'cause Beau was gone and I hadn't slept and Davis had called me a whore and someone finally saw how much I did up at that house.

"Oh honey," Jack said. "I'm so sorry."

I swiped at my face. "It's nothing," I told him. "I just want my brother back. 'Scuse me."

That coffee was still brewing, so I got up and walked to the side porch. They couldn't ask me to pour coffee that hadn't brewed yet. I went out the door and sat on the steps. The stars were bright and far away, but that swamp was slick-black. I'd be out there soon. I wouldn't leave til dawn, but I was going into that swamp, and I was going alone. Like I said, plenty of men went in and never came out, and plenty of men who did come out never talked about what they saw there. If they did talk about it, they talked in whispers, and they were afraid.

Growing up, you heard all the same stupid stories: there're gators about as long as school buses in the deep swamp and gar the size of VW Bugs—it was always VW Bugs. They said the feral hogs grew as big as ponies and they'd chase you down for meat. Cottonmouths thick as a man's thigh. There were coral snakes, too—we had a rhyme: Red on yellow, kill a fellow. Red on black, friend to Jack. That's how you tell them apart—by their stripes. A rattler or cottonmouth bite might make you wanna die, but you'll pull through unless you're especially small or sick or allergic to the antivenin they give you. Those pretty little coral snakes will kill you dead before you make it to the hospital.

Everyone knew those stories weren't the end. Something else brooded deep in that swamp, where trees stretched taller than watchtowers and water stood stagnant and dark. We didn't understand it—it wasn't for us to understand, any more than ants can understand us. And if you walked in, it decided if you walked out again.

Someone touched my shoulder as I stared down that blackness and I almost screamed.

"Hey, sweetie. I got worried about you out here alone," said Bam-Bam.

"I'm fine," I told him, but I sniffled hard.

"Baby girl, we'll find your brother."

I drew my knees up tight to my chest.

"It's been a bad night for you, hasn't it? Your littlest brother's missing and Quentin's in the sheriff's car, and I heard that sonofabitch yelling at you. I know you're not like he says."

They'd heard. I'd hoped they hadn't.

"You're not like the rest of them, Lila. Jack had it right."

I dropped my head down 'cause it was coming and I couldn't stop it. They were so predictable. Of course, Bam-Bam started to rub my back. I humped it up and cringed, but he didn't notice, or if he noticed, he didn't care. Which is worse, I wondered.

"You're different, Lila," he said and his hand went up and down, up and down.

It was like reading a script, and I was done with their scripts. I'd sworn I was, then I'd served those men coffee 'cause they planted their asses in my mother's kitchen. But I was done for real, and I shoved Bam-Bam's hand off me.

"Leave me alone," I told him. "I am different. I really don't like guys and even if I did, I wouldn't like you."

"Huh?" His face dropped into confusion.

"I mean I'd rather go out with your sister, dumbass," I said as I stood up.

"What?"

"I like girls, asshole."

He smirked. "Do you?"

I drew up taller. "Yeah, I do. You got a problem with that?"

"Not if I get to watch."

I pushed past him and strode back into the house. It was, I guess, the best I could've hoped for. Quentin leaned against the counter, hands dangling numbly in front of him.

"Sheriff Irwin let me out." He sounded three days of tired.

I made myself a cup of coffee. Quentin tried to make himself one, but his hands were clumsy and stupid. "I'll do it," I said, and fixed it for him.

Ed muttered something. Garth muttered back. In my own kitchen. They had no shame. "What'd you say?" I asked.

"Poor wittle baby's hands hurt?" Ed spoke in a high voice.

I was done with them and done with their scripts. I was finished with all of it.

"Your hands would hurt too if they were cuffed all night," I told him. "You're sitting at my kitchen table, asshole. Show some respect or get out."

"'Scuse me?" said Bam-Bam as he came in. "What was that?"

"Show some respect or get out," I told him. "Get off your ass and find my brother."

Quentin touched my arm. "Lila."

I slid away from him. "You heard me. You know damn well where Beau is. You're scared to go in there."

Their faces didn't move. They wouldn't say yes, but they wouldn't say no, either. I'd hit something beyond their joking. It wasn't calling

Quentin a sissy in our own kitchen 'cause his hands hurt like hell, and it wasn't one more crack about useless Carsons and their crazy mother and their clogged-up gutters. Those things mattered—they mattered the way that every Joiner in town was poor as dirt, or a Leonard boy was as likely to jump your car as steal your tires.

You could joke about those things. You could turn them over and look at them and laugh. But that swamp was a whole 'nother matter. We stood on its unknowable edges and lived in an uneasy peace: whatever brooded there would stay there, and in exchange, we'd stay out, or at least out of its way. Out of its business, whatever that business might be.

No man at that table would say he wasn't scared.

Jack Richardson stood. "Lookit you all dressed up for an adventure. You think you're gonna go out and find him yourself?"

"Maybe I will," I said.

"That's for us to do," Jack told me. He didn't bother to push his chair in. "You should have your pretty little ass in this kitchen making coffee. Your mama lets you run wild."

Our dishwasher hummed. Most of the men leaned on their elbows in front of coffee mugs. A few kept Coke cans they used as spit-cups. They'd never chew tobacco in the kitchen if Mama was awake. Ed Hines and Mike Harner's daddy propped themselves against the marble countertop.

"I thought you said I was different from my brothers," I told him. "Or am I just different 'cause you got something you wanna use to shut my mouth, Jack? You think I didn't hear you outside?"

"Someone oughta shut your mouth," he said. "Don't matter how they do it."

Quentin touched my arm again. "Lila."

"I'm just waiting until sunrise," I told them. "You think I'm gonna stand in here and wait for you useless fucks to find my brother? You think he's not worth a damn 'cause he's a Carson and worse than that, you think he doesn't matter 'cause he ain't right."

I said the last part in the worst hick accent I could manage. Quentin's hand closed over my arm. "You're not going out there, Lila."

"I'm leaving in a few," I said. "I need to get some things."

No one spoke as I leaned against my own counter and sipped coffee. I didn't know what might be waiting for me—it seemed too awful for my imagination to hold. I couldn't think about it. I could only walk toward it. I finished my coffee, rinsed my mug, and set it by the sink. It was maybe six o'clock, and Mama was asleep. Davis was asleep. I went into my room, locked the door, and wrote a note.

I wouldn't find Beau in that swamp. I really believed that. There was too much land out there, a vast quagmire of water and earth stretching ten miles west to the Congaree River, and who knew how far north and south—and that was assuming he'd gone west, not east, where the swamp still stretched another several miles, and that he wasn't hiding in one of the smaller pockets of swamp tucked between Lower Congaree's highways and hummocks. I'd get lost, and I wouldn't come out.

But Mama had Davis-the-heir, and she had Quentin-the-spare. I was for her, but since she had my brothers, the swamp taking me didn't mean much. Hopefully one of those men would find Beau, but they probably wouldn't. At least I wouldn't be around to know it. I didn't wanna see the slow-moving horror of his disappearance: those hours stretching into days of lost hope, then that moment when Sheriff Irwin scaled back the search and announced they were searching for a body, not a boy. I didn't wanna plan any funeral, much less a funeral without a casket, and I didn't wanna walk through our silent house and pick up Beau's toys one last time.

A better person would've looked those things in the face and lived with them.

I couldn't tell them the other reasons, either. I couldn't say: I will not be Miss Legare County for you. You will never hand me roses and stand me on a fire engine at the Lower Congaree Firefly Festival. Davis thinks that makes me a whore and Quentin thinks that he can keep me safe as long as I stay his. Those men in the kitchen tried to tell me I was different so they could get something from me. They'll try everything they can to get it, and they'll keep trying until I pick one of them or get the hell out. If I don't, they'll lose patience and take what they want. When they do that, no one will stop them 'cause I'm a Carson. I couldn't say those things to Mama and Quentin.

I couldn't think too hard about what that swamp taking me might mean, either. So when I tried to write a note, I only came up with: I love you. I will do my best to find Beau. Please take care of yourselves and please stay safe. Love, Lila.

Quentin would find that note, and he'd blame himself. I hated that and I didn't. He was as bad as Davis and he deserved it. "They'll hurt you," he said. "They only want one thing and they'll hurt you for it, Lila."

"I won't let them," I told him. "I'll stop them." We were standing in my bedroom. It was April, and the tree frogs were screeching their rainy night love songs. That swamp scent drifted in my open windows, that terrible smell that drew you in even if you hated it.

"You won't be able to stop them. They're bigger and stronger than you." Quentin picked up my wrist and circled it with his thumb and finger. It was a strange thing for him to do, and I flushed like I had so long before when he said I should wear a bra. "See? I don't want them to hurt you. I love you and it scares me so much."

"You can't keep me locked up," I said. "I'm gonna see guys sometimes."

I was careful. I said sometimes 'cause I didn't lie to Quentin.

"Once in a while, you say this stuff, Lila. I don't know what to think." He looked at me and I wasn't sure if I saw a question or something darker and broken. He still held my wrist. I was wearing my regular pajamas: a sports bra, a tank top and sleepy pants. He'd seen me in them every day of our lives, but I suddenly felt like crossing my arms over my chest.

"I don't know what you mean, that you don't know what to think," I told him. I was still careful. I didn't say it but I said it.

He turned my wrist over. "I think they'll hurt you, Lila. I think they'll hurt you 'cause you're beautiful."

Quentin's gaze was odd and jagged, and when I tried to pull my wrist away his grip tightened. "They'll hurt you for other reasons, too," he told me. "You can't."

I yanked harder. "I can," I said. "I can be whoever I am."

"You can't. Stop it." He grabbed my other wrist. "Stop it, Lila."

"Goddammit Quentin," I told him."Let me go."

"You can't."

"I can so."

"No you can't, Lila, I swear to God you can't."

"Fucking let me go."

"You can't."

"I said let me go dammit."

He pinned my wrists in one hand and grabbed my chin. Quentin made me look him in the face. "You absolutely cannot," he said, and I saw that deep-rooted madness in him. I knew it like I knew how to smile and say Bless your heart, but I'd never imagined it in him. "Lila, don't you understand they'll hurt you for it faster than they'll hurt you for being beautiful?" he asked. "They'll only think it's better, 'cause you're both."

When I tried to twist away, he wouldn't let me.

"I wouldn't hurt you," he said. "I'd never hurt you."

"You are hurting me," I told him. "Let me go."

"I won't hurt you," Quentin said. "You're too pretty to hurt. You're perfect. I won't hurt you, then I'll make sure none of them ever can."

I chose my words very carefully. "I am saying no," I told him. "No. If I say no and you still do there's a name for that."

"Don't be ugly." He was very quiet and his thumb on my chin petted back and forth, back and forth. "You don't have to be ugly about it. I love you. You're too perfect for them."

"I am telling you no," I said again. Quentin still held my wrists tight.

"I love you and I won't hurt you. I swear I wouldn't hurt you. They'd still want that one thing, but they could never have it, Lila. I'd keep you safe. That other stuff wouldn't even matter anymore."

He had my wrists trapped tight and my chin wrenched up. I had to stare down that son-of- the-South sanctity or close my eyes. This was my own twin who loved me, and he meant everything. I couldn't get away.

So I stopped fighting and disappeared into one of those melty-soft girls they all wanted for their own. "I love you too," I said. "I love you so much, Q. You would never, ever hurt me 'cause you love me."

His hand slid from my chin to my cheek. "See," he said. "You understand." I blinked so slowly as I nodded. "I understand."

Quentin let go of my wrist. He cupped my face, and I had to hold his eyes as his knuckles stroked my cheek. I had to stay sweet, and I couldn't look away. I thought I'd lose it. I almost wanted to lose it, 'cause then it wouldn't be real, and I could say, this did not happen. But I stayed sugar-sweet to get through it. I waited, and oh God, I didn't want to see him like that.

I waited until he leaned down, then I flew back and slammed against my bedroom wall.

"You fucking rapist," I said as I plastered myself against something solid. A poster crackled behind me. "You're a goddamn rapist. Get out or I'll scream."

Quentin's face dropped into confusion. "But you said—"

"I said no. I told you I said no. Get out or I'll scream."

"You told me you understood." He actually teared up, that bastard. "I love you and I don't want you to get hurt, and if—"

"I am counting to three, and if you're still here I'll scream, and when Mama comes, I'll tell," I said. "One."

"I love you."

"Two."

"Lila, please."

"Don't make me do it. I'll tell."

"I don't want them to, I want you to be safe—"

I opened my mouth, and Quentin slammed the door behind him as he ran. I curled with my back against it, and I cried for a long, long time. He was my best friend. I loved him. I hated him more than I'd ever hated anyone. There was nowhere else to go and nowhere else to be.

Finally I pulled my dresser in front of the door, but I never went to sleep. I stopped trying at five in the morning and got dressed for school, then finished my homework. There wasn't another choice.

Leaving my room choked me. I knew what waited outside. I knew its face and its voice and its logical end. But I made myself leave anyway. Is this what happened to Mama? I wondered. Did she see it and she couldn't unsee it? They made her Miss Legare County. I ran my hand over our pretty wallpaper, old like everything else in our house. Did she learn it when she was my age or did she learn it later? Did she learn it from Daddy?

Quentin was eating breakfast in an empty kitchen.

He didn't lift his head. "I didn't go to sleep," he said. "I shouldn't—"

"Don't you ever," I said. "Don't you ever say anything like that again, and don't you ever mention it again. I mean ever, d'you understand me?"

Quentin nodded at his cereal bowl.

"Don't you ever." I started to cry then. He got up like he meant to hug me, but I ran. I ran from that house, ran out the door to an old tobacco barn, and I sobbed alone. There was too much to say. There were old uniforms in the attic, and Mama haunted our house like a ghost. She was Miss Legare County, I could've told Quentin. They took her picture and handed her roses, and she rode on top of a fire engine in the Lower Congaree Firefly Festival on the Fourth of July. An heir and a spare and one for her, and Daddy said she did good. That's what you want to do me and I won't let you.

We'd turned eighteen the week before, and I loved Quentin. I hated him. There was nowhere else to go, d'you understand? I'd lost him. I knew that old princess-in-the-tower story. But I never imagined it would wear his face.

Chapter Six

2019

I sat up in bed. Lila's voice hadn't wavered. She still watched her ceiling instead of me, and her hair still tumbled on her overly large pile of pillows. But her arms had slipped down to hug herself as she spoke, and she'd pulled her quilt to her chin.

"Do you want me to get you some clothes?" I kept my voice gentle.

Lila flipped to face me. "No, thank you. That's very sweet of you, though." Her knees drew toward her chest; that quilt stayed at her chin. "I'm fine."

Slowly, careful not to startle, I reached toward her. When she merely watched me, I tucked her hair behind her ear. "Did it come out of nowhere?" I asked. "It seems like it did."

Lila seemed to think. "It did and it didn't. Quentin was always saying guys would hurt me and they only wanted one thing. But if Davis was around, he'd say yeah, they do, you've gotta be careful. So that part yes. But I didn't think..." Lila curled a little tighter.

"Quentin really thought he was keeping me safe. That's what I'm trying to explain, McKenzie."

I focused on her dresser, a curving Art Nouveau antique with curly inlay. It matched her vanity. "He thought he was keeping you safe," I said. "By sleeping with you."

"I know that sounds like the most messed-up thing in the world," Lila told me. "But if I was his I wouldn't be anyone else's. I'd still be perfect."

I didn't want to say her twin sounded like a serial killer, so I didn't answer.

"It wasn't him, McKenzie. Don't you understand?" Pleading, maybe worry, seeped into Lila's tone, and I combed my fingers through her hair until she uncurled. "They expect things. There are certain things to say and certain things to do, and there are certain things you never say and certain things you never do. I'd said one of those things to Quentin, and I'd told him I would do one of them."

"You mean sleep with a girl." I kept playing with her hair. "That was part of it. But the other thing was part of it, too."

"Did he think he could cure you?!"

She tensed again, and I petted her head. Slowly, she seemed to calm down. "Quentin did the math. If one of those men had—had done anything to me, no one would care. He was trying to minimize the damage. If I could stay perfect, in his mind, I'd stay safe."

"I don't—I mean—"

"You don't understand." Lila pushed herself up, but took the quilt with her. "It wasn't Quentin. It was all of them. But it came for me as Quentin, and that was the gut punch. I loved Quentin."

Her verb tense caught me. "What do you mean, 'loved'?"

Lila settled back onto her pillows. "I'll get there," she said, "if you still want me to."

"I do," I said. "Don't stop."

She rearranged her quilt and spoke again.

CHAPTER SEVEN

2016

When I came down with my backpack, Quentin was cleaning the kitchen alone.

"They're talking to the sheriff." He moved from mug to sink to dishwasher, his hair greasy from lack of sleep. His hands still seemed stiff and painful.

I didn't answer.

"You're going out there." Quentin didn't break his rhythm between the sink and the dishwasher and the mugs. Our yellow kitchen light seemed warm and familiar as an early morning, and those coffee mugs broke my heart with a tenderness that comes from the everyday.

I waited a long time then I said, "Yes."

"I'd try to talk you out of it, but I can't," Quentin told me. He didn't lift his head. "We don't talk anymore. I know it's my fault. I thought—"

I closed my eyes. "Quentin don't."

Water ran into the quiet between us. "Are you ready for whatever's out there?" he asked.

I wasn't and I couldn't lie to my twin. It watched and it waited and it wanted. I knew only that much, and I didn't want to know anymore. My stomach rolled.

"I'm gonna find Beau," I said.

"It won't let you if it doesn't want him found."

"Then I'll ask for him back." I turned to go.

He caught my hand. "I love you," Quentin said. "Please remember that I love you, and if I made mistakes that's why I made them."

"I know," I told him, and I left the kitchen. My boots sounded on that cypress hardwood as I passed through the mudroom and walked out the back door. I couldn't say goodbye to him, not for the last time. It would've hurt too bad, and I had to pretend I was coming back. I thought then there were right words to say and I was too scared to say them. Now I know that sometimes words break apart under their own weight and there's nothing to say at all.

The deputies kicked pebbles and spit tobacco and waited for Sheriff Irwin, who was talking on his radio again. An early-morning fog wrapped our fields in gray, and trees rose from the mist, half-seen sentinels who would not desert their posts. I could've stayed and listened to the sheriff's plans. I thought about it. I could go where no one else was going, and I'd have a better chance of finding Beau.

I took in the sullen, unmoving fog. Those men would go two-by-two with chattering radios, and they'd stick to the swamp's easy edges. Deep muck or creeks would stop them. They'd go in far enough to say they tried and they would come back. They'd do it every day until there was no hope.

They had wives and kids and they wouldn't leave them for a useless Carson, especially for that changeling boy who didn't count. They wouldn't go deep enough to risk anything, and they wouldn't find Beau.

But I was his sister, and I loved him. I felt something behind that mist, and it felt different, as if it were examining me or sizing me up. I would walk as far as I could. I wouldn't stop. I had resigned myself: I would not come out. It wouldn't let me. But instead of giving up I had to find Beau. No one else would do it for a useless changeling. He didn't count. I didn't count either. They could make me Miss Legare County; they could make me a princess in a tower or they could make me a whore. But I didn't matter.

Maybe that's what gave me enough courage to fade from that clump of deputies, those men who'd laughed about shutting my mouth then asked me to pour their coffee, those men who wouldn't risk anything for my brother, and walk to the edge of our field. Dew soaked my boots. The sun had scribbled the sky in pinks and golds, but it hadn't risen above the treeline. Our land stayed dim, shadow deepening to darker shadow.

I looked one last time. Our white-columned house rose from monochrome fields. Its shutters needed nailed straight and Mama had closed off the fourth floor, but it still stood. Daddy's office was locked. Mama and Davis were sleeping. In our yellow-lit kitchen, Quentin stepped through that same dance from mug to sink to dishwasher. He would do it until it was done. Plants grew from our gutters.

What did Beau think of our house, which still stood through the swamp's slow swallowing? What did he see when he watched from its windows?

I faced the ashen, grooved trunks of bald cypress trees, then stepped from lush grass into leaf litter. One step took me in. Three steps and those trees closed behind me. The deputies' noise dulled, then disappeared, and my feet fell silent on a deer track's root-rutted dirt. No insects hummed, and no birds sang. A lone crow rose from a bare branch and was gone. That mist clung low and heavy, funereal, and sweet decay hung in its wake. I lifted my head and looked as far as I could. Trees faded to greens and grays, and then to a dimmed haze of nothing. That nothing chilled me. It watched and it waited and it wanted. Those cypresses and tupelos and swamp oaks loomed wide and tall as living steeples, while smaller trees, the dogwoods and hollies, grew stunted, spindled and afraid. Only I moved and it bided its time. I was coming. It could wait.

I called Beau's name. The swamp stole my voice.

Thorned smilax vines lined the small track. I'd hold back one, and another would catch my pants, then I'd sidestep a third and another would lash me. Blood beaded my scratched hands. I walked in that strange quiet, past cypress knees rearing from stale water, through sinks gone into wet muck that sucked at my boots. I stopped on a higher hummock, where I stood on leaves shredded with time and water risen, then fallen again. Silently, another crow dipped off a limb and disappeared. Spanish moss cobwebbed on high-hanging branches, but everything stooped low under those swamp-giants, the cypresses and tupelos. Broad-leafed brush grew between shallow black pools. Everything ran to green and gray, brown and black— even fallen logs decayed under gray and brown turkey-tail fungus. My red blood was bright and sharp. Nothing moved, and in that stagnant silence, I heard my heart's frail but endless throb, on and on and on.

It pushed closer. I'd've shivered if I hadn't gone so still. The humidity was its own hot breath on my neck. It was waiting.

"Let him be okay," I said, and slapped my bloody hand against a cypress trunk. Red smeared on gray; my words bloomed and spread in that long quiet. "Let Beau be okay and I'll give anything."

I waited.

I didn't know what I was waiting for—what sign or signal or testament, what suggestion of a deal brokered or bought. I would've recognized it when it came. Nothing came. I drank, and I began walking through those muddy dips again. Sometimes puddles stretched over my path and I had to pick my way through them, sloshing and praying I didn't slip, praying they didn't drop too deep. I shattered that silence again and again with my brother's name.

That sun never rose—of course it rose, but in that mossed cathedral created by whatever waits, I saw only branches meeting overhead and sometimes a colorless sky above. Maybe the swamp was that waiting thing's bent vision of beauty. Vines twined up tree trunks, vines thicker than thighs, some black and hairy—those were poison ivy—and others gnarled and woody and old. My game track forked and twisted and once in a while disappeared altogether. Then I stopped and waited for a reason to choose one way over another. I never asked out loud but I waited. At first I thought a sign would come, that whatever watched and waited would reach down and say: There. That way. But I saw nothing and I heard nothing. I found a compass in that old backpack, and I tried checking it, but it spun uselessly. Where is my brother, I tried thinking instead. Tell me where Beau is. But one way seemed no better than another. The swamp was a labyrinth I navigated blind.

But I had to pick so I picked and kept walking. I called Beau's name again, again, again.

Around midday, I found a dark, wide creek. Its black water ran in swift rills, and it twisted between low-hanging cypresses, then off into the distance. I couldn't see two inches through it, but I stopped and rolled my pants. I kept my boots on; that backpack had a first aid kit with blister patches if wet shoes wore my skin raw, but I might step on anything under that black water. I hoped I wouldn't have to swim. Beau could've made it across that creek easy—those damn deputies wouldn't've understood that. They'd've thought a kid like him, he wouldn't dare get in and if he did, well, they were looking for a body, not a boy. But Beau could swim better than any kid I ever saw. I straightened up. Roots made me a muddy staircase down, and I grabbed for brush to keep my footing.

Something rose from the black water.

I scrabbled up that bank so quick I can't recall doing it. Decayed leaves clung to an immense back, then slid off as water streamed over hard scales. It surfaced without a sound; only the creek broke the swamp-quiet as it heaved toward air and light: a gator too long to live, too big to breathe, with a pupil slit like a snake's. It should've been black as that water, but it was white and fat as a grub under a log, like it had never seen the sun and never would. I backed up farther.

If I'd've stepped into that water it would've had me.

But it didn't want me. As long as it was, long as a car and fat with swamp-leavings, fish and nutria and probably deer, it could've lunged. It could've dragged me under and bit, then held me there until I drowned and made me part of that place. But it just watched me with that eye red as the blood I'd smacked on that cypress bark. I didn't move, and it didn't move, and we blinked at each other in that gray place where the water ran black. When I slid a foot back, it sank slowly. It would go down and rest silent in its darkness. Far from the bank, I unrolled my pants, drank, and walked on. When the creek wound away, I didn't follow.

I didn't worry that white gator had taken Beau. I knew it hadn't, and I didn't know why. I chewed my lip as smilax tore at me. I knew that gator hadn't touched Beau the way I knew Beau had walked into the swamp. I pressed my lips together and stopped where my path met another. Where is my brother, I asked again, and when no answer came, I picked a way and kept going.

The landscape didn't change. If I saw a bird, it was a crow, and it was silent. The trunks were gray and the leaves were green and something old watched me. Fungus bloomed on fallen logs. I drank and walked and yelled my brother's name. Nothing answered. I should've brought food, but I hadn't thought of it—thirst caught quick, but hunger was a slow-gnawing need, and I hadn't expected to live long enough for it. I'd expected, instead, that white alligator. I'd expected the feral hogs whose tracks dotted my path, who'd rooted up whole hummocks of earth. I'd expected things unknown and unimagined, slavering creatures of the deep swamp that no one lived to tell about. I'd never expected my own rumbling stomach.

I'd thought that swamp would have animals beyond the deformed alligator and a few hog-leavings. But no deer crashed in the underbrush. No squirrels chattered in the deep leaf litter. Nothing rustled from far away, and that was worse than hearing a sound and wondering what it could be. A sound might've scared me, but I wouldn't've been alone. I wasn't alone, I decided as that thing watched, shivering my spine, you were never alone in those woods, but beasts hid from man, and that swamp-forest hid from me. The gator had risen from black water, but it had risen to stop my path, and it had sunk again. What snakes twisted through those vines?

I walked and called, walked and called. My feet hurt even in good hiking boots, and my back began to ache. My watch died. That place threw no telltale shadows to read east or west or noon or after. But when the light dimmed, I felt sunset in my bones. I found a patch of higher ground and checked for snakes—kicked and stomped and brushed my feet in circles like it would've made a difference. I cleared a space in the brush and hunkered into it. Beau would be curled up in the brush, alone, like me. But I was eighteen and I could stand being by myself. I remembered him crying and banging that door while Mama stood there ignoring him.

What if he was lonely? I couldn't sneak into his room and take his hand. I couldn't say, D'you wanna sleep in my room, Beau? My throat lumped up as I huddled in the dead leaves. It was bad to think of my baby brother on cold ground, and it was bad to think of him hungry, but it was worst to think of him scared and alone in the dark. My throat hurt and my eyes filled and I tried hard not to cry—I wouldn't please whatever watched and waited by giving in to that misery.

It wound down the game track maybe ten minutes later. The forest was deepening gray but it was sleek-black, a beautiful danger of a cat with a tufted tail. There are no lions east of the Mississippi, they say. There are no cougars and there are no black panthers. You can read that—everything says it, but everything also says that people glimpse them, these pieces of a landscape yet unbroken, out of time and out of place but still persisting. They see them and they swear: It wasn't a pet cat, it wasn't a bobcat, it was a panther and a black one, too. Once they lived on the ragged edges of our night terrors and they live on. I know. I saw.

That wild piece of the swamp slunk by my nest of brush. Its paws padded soundlessly. Then it stopped. It looked back, and it looked at me.

That panther waited, and we stayed there for a long time. Then it flicked its long, black tail and leapt suddenly to a fallen tree, where it sat like an enormous housecat. Its tail twitched and those wide yellow eyes stared me down. I found myself standing. Whatever waited swelled and shoved near. Nausea rose. It was coming. The panther dropped to the faint trail, then slid into the gloom-gray swamp.

It wanted me to follow. If I didn't follow through that dropping dark, it would turn its claws and bright-white teeth on me—I knew that like I knew my own name. So I walked. My eyes adjusted as night swallowed the swamp. It was hot but I hugged myself, and I didn't stop. I wanted my brother back. Please let my brother be okay, I said over and over. Let my brother be okay and I will give anything. I just want to find Beau. Please let me find Beau, I begged that ancient thing that waited. Please make my brother be okay. That trail led me deeper and I pleaded in that night-silence. No forest should keep silent at night. My footfalls seemed too loud and their sound traveled too far—anything could hear them and anything could be hidden behind those tangling vines. I heard my heart beat too fast. That waiting thing heard my heart, too.

Think of Beau, I told myself. Think of him and not whatever's waiting out there. But it panted hot against my neck, and when vines swiped me I leapt at its touch. Remember Beau, I thought. You love Beau and you can't stop, even if you are following a black panther that might tear into you and whatever waits is close enough to snatch you up.

I wondered why it didn't. I felt sick while I begged for my brother. Where was it leading me? I thought maybe I should stop and let the panther do its work. If I turned around it would take me quick and clean, one long leap onto my back and those knife-bright teeth would snap my neck. It would be fast, and it would be painless, or at least mostly painless, and I'd escape whatever terror waited at the end of that trail. I thought hard about it. I really did.

I was almost choking-scared, but I wanted to find my baby brother. That ancient thing was close—I could've tugged that panther's tail-tuft. I might've been terrified but I remembered Beau crying on the other side of that door and I made myself put one foot in front of the other. I will give anything, I thought over and over. Anything.

As the track curved, that panther arched away. The trees parted and I stopped. A blackwater creek rushed quick and wide; across it, a fire sprang high. It threw wild, wheeling shadows, over the tupelos and oak, swamp-shadows flaring in feral exultation. That savage imp-dance could've snatched me up, and God knows what might've happened if it had. Half-gone in it, I almost threw myself into that orange-and-yellow shimmered water. Instead my chest went hollow and I stepped back. I could've collapsed like a doll.

My baby brother sat behind the bright flames, and that fire flared in Beau's eyes. Cottonmouths coiled his thin, bare shoulders. They wrapped his skinny arms like rings and curled in his lap like cats. Fire shone on their scales, black against his moon-pale skin. Beau held a coral snake in his hands, red-yellow-black, and that small, thin snake twined endlessly between his fingers.

I thought I'd find him curled by a tree or tucked next to a fallen log; I thought I'd find him small and scared. I'd find a scrap of a boy who needed water and rescue and extra arms to carry him home. Instead that night ghost of a panther slipped behind my brother and dropped to the earth. Beau settled against it like an old friend; he didn't watch me but the panther did.

"Beau!" I shouted. My voice cracked over that splashing water and snapping fire. It was too out of place there, and I knew when I called that it didn't belong. "Beau!"

His fire-shining eyes met mine.

I tried to say, You have to come home, Mama misses you. Or, It's time to go now. I struggled for something to offer my naked, firelit brother, but nothing came, and I had no words for that child wrapped in snakes. I stared instead. And as I stared I realized he wasn't the little boy Mama wouldn't take to the doctor or the silent thing Miz Leonard called a changeling. It almost broke me to look.

No one ever asked Beau what he wanted, and if they did ask, they answered for him. They did what they were gonna do, and they did it no matter if he liked it or not. He'd reached for Quentin before we left for school, but Quentin said, No Beau. Even Quentin who loved him talked as if he were an inconvenience. So did I, and my chest clutched. I saw him but I didn't. I played his animal shows, but I'd never wondered why he loved them. We left Beau with Davis 'cause it was easy, and Davis ditched him 'cause he wanted to work. Beau could want things, but he only got them if they were easy to give.

I saw all of that at once and it almost drove me to my knees. That was my baby brother's whole life but I had never understood it.

He'd finally run from it.

But when he ran, my baby brother ran the wrong way. He ran from our broken-shuttered house to whatever waited out here. It had called him to itself, and when he finally came it snatched him up. Whatever watched and waited had gobbled my baby brother and made him part of itself.

He wasn't that sad little boy anymore. But he wasn't Beau, either. Black mud smeared his cheeks and twigs tangled in his curls. The swamp had recreated Beau in its image. He belonged to it then. He'd run away to become himself, and the swamp had swallowed him.

He set the snake in his lap and rested a hand on the panther's broad head.

"You understand," he said, and he didn't need words. "That's why we let you see, because you understand."

Nothing here would hurt him. Nothing would touch him.

I'd found Beau. I'd been given what I asked for and my heart hit my throat: I'd never asked to bring him home. I'd said let me find him, let him be okay, I'll give anything. I never said let me bring my brother out.

Beau's face flattened suddenly. "Leave," he was saying, and he didn't need words any more than he'd needed them when he cried on the other side of his bedroom door. He wasn't that locked-up little boy anymore, but he wasn't himself, either. He'd made a choice and gone away. When he'd grabbed at freedom, whatever brooded here had broken him. That was the worst part. It had taken him as soon as he ran from our swamp-swallowed house.

"Get out of this place," the child was saying. "This is not for you." I ran.

CHAPTER EIGHT

"I know how it sounds." Lila spoke toward her ceiling. "But I saw him."

"I believe you." I threaded my fingers through her hair. Maybe I believed her then. Maybe I didn't. I knew that stories could tell more truth than facts. "How far out there did you go?"

Lila shifted on her old sheets. "I was gone for a day and a night."

I fit myself around her. "I'm sorry," I replied. I had nothing else to offer, and I let those words stand for those that failed me.

Her chest rose suddenly, then fell. "I don't know how I got out of there. It's blurry. I ran most of the way, and I didn't retrace my steps. I was—I was pushed out."

Lila's sheets were soft. She was warm; her antique lights glowed red-dim behind my eyelids. "I'm sorry about your brother," I told her again. My lips brushed her skin while I spoke. "I'm glad you got out."

An old heater rattled. I cuddled her close, but she stayed tense against me. "I'm not," she replied.

"You're not what?"

"I'm not glad I got out." Lila drew another long, shuddered breath.

I bit my lip. "You found your brother. I thought—"

"I'm not finished," she said.

Chapter Nine

2016

I tasted smoke before I smelled it. I'd been running for a long time and my sides hurt; my chest ached and I was gulping air when that strange tang hit my dried-out tongue. My world had narrowed to a single point: I had to get out and I had to get out fast. The swamp and whatever brooded in it was shoving me hard. I'd never run so far and my lungs caught in a wheeze just short of a sob, like a kid who'd cried too hard for too long. That odd taste took me a second to place, but when I did, I forced myself to run faster. Smilax tore at me. I hurdled over logs and my feet squelched in mud that didn't squish but splattered instead. It caked my pants and dotted my shirt, and when I swiped at sweat, it streaked my face.

The smoke taste grew stronger as the distance smeared gray rather than black. My eyes stung. I'd been hurling through darkness with only my flashlight to stop me from slamming cypress knees or tumbling over logs. That black was dulling, but ahead of me it turned into real gray, dawn-gray, unfiltered by tree branches, and I was almost there. When I reached the treeline, I fell to the wet grass of our field and convulsed into hacking. Smoke tears streamed down my face.

My house was on fire.

Flames devoured it from top to bottom. They seethed over the battered roof and flared from broken-shuttered windows; fire climbed its once-white columns. It peeled the paint and charred them to black and they wouldn't stand much longer. Those plant-clogged gutters were gone. I choked and squinted. I couldn't get up. I couldn't run to help and for a long time, I could only lie on that dew-covered grass and suck air in hard shudders. I had to watch it burn.

Beau's fire crackled. My house thundered. You think of a fire's heat but you never think of its sound, and a fire that big is as loud as the Lord's own judgment. Eventually I forced myself up and reeled toward my front door. I could try to find Quentin. But as I stumbled closer the flames grew hotter, too hot to stand. They slammed me back when I came thirty feet from the house. Maybe Quentin and the rest of them were in the back. I staggered around but the flames leapt higher; that fire writhed like snakes, like those cottonmouths in my brother's lap, and then I knew. I had promised anything.

I yanked my hair back—I had a tie around my wrist and if my hair caught I'd be good as dead. I set my jaw and ran. At first that heat hit like an open oven, then a bad sunburn, and then it became almost unbearable as I kicked the back door open, dropped to my belly, and crawled into the kitchen. Smoke swirled thick and hot; the air wasn't air at all, but a soup more ash than oxygen, and breathing it seemed like breathing through tar. Shapes sprawled over the floor, and a second passed before I realized they were men. My vision blurred and my lungs ached and I didn't have long or I wouldn't come out again. But one of those bodies had chin-length hair. I was almost out of time but I grabbed his arm and dragged. It took everything. Oh

God, it took everything I had left, and those last few yards I couldn't breathe at all—there was no air and I thought I might collapse right inside my own back door. But I yanked hard and I pulled myself along on my elbows and we were out. I let myself gasp for a few moments then I half-stood and towed him free of the fire. Maybe he'd make it and maybe he wouldn't but I'd gotten him out.

Far from the house, I dropped next to him. Quentin was alive. The deputies' cars were empty. Sparks rushed over them and caught their sensitive parts, their rubber gaskets or tires or fabric seats—no one closed their windows on hot nights in Lower Congaree. Soon the cars were charring, then burning, that terrible sick rubber-char that turns the stomach and throws up oily black smoke. My house roared and spat, and something inside boomed, an explosive structural crash that sent the whole conflagration shuddering and collapsing inward with its own weight. I had promised.

Stray ash caught the barn, and fire gobbled at that old wood, its nooks and crannies stuffed with hay. It wouldn't last long and I could only hope the grass stayed wet enough to stop a wildfire. Smoke rose in rolling plumes that spread and bloomed in the paling sky. Day had broken and the sun had risen behind thick clouds. I couldn't do anything more. I had promised and I had paid, and I'd managed to drag Quentin clear. I curled next to him. The house burned, burned. Now I had nothing so they could call me anything. It didn't matter.

I was shivering cold when the fire trucks came. I never figured out how they made it—maybe the fire tower spotted smoke. They barreled down our drive with sirens on and they didn't notice Quentin and me right away. I couldn't talk at first—I tried but no words came. My throat hurt too bad and when I tried to force it my lungs burned.

They told me that an ambulance was coming, but before it got there, they did things to Quentin's burns and wrapped me in one of those shock blankets. It was Wednesday morning. They took a long, long time to put that fire out and I watched it all. I had promised anything.

"Where's the sheriff?" the fire chief asked me. "He's supposed to be out here."

"I just got here," I said. My voice scratched and talking hurt bad. "I was trying to find Beau and came in from the swamp. The house was on fire and no one was here."

Chief Sunderland went white. I didn't think people actually did that but I saw it happen. His red cheeks actually paled. "Sheriff Irwin and at least five deputies are supposed to be out here right now," he told me. "Their cars, they're still here."

Except they weren't cars anymore, they were shells, and they were smoking now that the men had put their fires out.

I stared at the pebbles instead of my own burnt house. The broken shutters didn't matter anymore. "When I got Quentin I saw bodies in the kitchen."

Chief Sunderland went quiet for a long time. "How many bodies, honey?"

"I saw a lot," I said, and somehow I wasn't crying. I'd made a deal. I'd made a promise and oh God, had I paid my part. They were all gone but Quentin, and he looked bad. He was burnt all over, and his breath wasn't right. It was long and shuddery and wheezing, and you could tell when you heard it that he might not make it, but I couldn't think about that. I couldn't think about Davis or Mama. Worst of all, I couldn't think of my baby brother. I couldn't think about what we'd done to him, and I couldn't think about how he'd finally run, only to be swallowed.

One ambulance took me to the hospital in Columbia, and another took Quentin. "Who should we call?" they asked when we got there. "Give us your grandparents' names, or aunts or uncles or godparents."

I huddled under my blanket. Who the hell could I call? My father was dead and now my mother was gone too; my grandparents had long ago died and my parents had been only children. "There isn't anybody to call," I told them.

Eventually, Chief Sunderland showed up, and he said since Estlin Lanier had been my father's law partner and Davis's godfather, they should call him. I hadn't seen Uncle Estlin in years, and he'd blurred into a red face and bright blond hair. I collapsed into sleep eventually. I don't remember much after that. Maybe it was that day or the next, or even the day after that, but I woke up to Uncle Estlin in my white hospital room. His wife Charlotte had come with him. She looked like a grown-up sorority girl, a little pudgy but with bouncy blonde hair and blue eyes. I was hooked up to oxygen and had more than a few burns but nothing that would scar bad, even if they hurt like hell. I'd never met Aunt Charlotte, but she sat on my bed and picked up my hand.

"I'm so sorry, Lila honey," she started.

"You don't have to tell me about Mama and Davis," I said. My voice rasped and it didn't sound like my own. "I already know."

"It was smoke inhalation," she told me. "They were in their beds."

At least they'd slept through it. At least they hadn't suffered. I held to that. I had pulled Quentin out and Mama and Davis hadn't suffered. Something wicked and dark as that night said they deserved it. I shoved it back. I didn't want to think about how we treated Beau and what that fire might have to do with it. I didn't want to think of my lost little brother at all. He was gone forever.

"What about Quentin?" I asked.

In the corner of my room, Uncle Estlin pressed his lips together and looked at his wife. He had brought her to absolve him from saying all the worst things.

84

"Quentin had a lot of oxygen deprivation," Aunt Charlotte told me. She spoke carefully, like she had to dance around the truth and tell me something without telling it. "Quentin's doctors aren't sure how he'll come out of it. He'll need a lot of skin grafts for his burns."

I nodded and turned to the wall. Justice would insist on itself. Mama and Davis were dead and I had lost everything, but Quentin had a special punishment. I didn't know what would happen after that. I didn't have a house and I didn't have parents. I had a year left of high school. I thought about it after Uncle Estlin and Aunt Charlotte left. Foster care, I figured. That would be a misery, but at least it would end. I didn't say anything about it when Aunt Charlotte came back with clothes for me.

"Thank you," I told her. "You didn't have to bring me these but I'm very grateful you did, ma'am."

"You'll need something to wear home," she told me. "The doctors told me you'll be ready to go tomorrow, and we can't let you come home naked, can we?" And she gave me a tiny smile, the kind of smile you give sad people.

I must've looked at her strange 'cause her eyes went wide and shocked. "Dear God Lila," she said. "You don't think we'd let you go anywhere else, do you?"

"Why would you take me home?" I asked. "I'm not who you think I am."

Her eyebrows met. "What d'you mean, sweetie?"

"I mean I like other girls." I'd seen my baby brother swallowed by that swamp, lit by fire and coiled with cottonmouths, and I'd dragged my twin from a burning house. An heir and a spare and me for Mama. I would not be for anyone anymore.

"I'm not Miss Legare County," I told Aunt Charlotte. "Everyone says Mama didn't raise me right and you know it but it wasn't her, it's me. She couldn't've raised me right if she tried."

Aunt Charlotte seemed to study me. That's it, I thought. You just had to keep your mouth shut for a few months, Lila. But you didn't and now you're fucked.

"You mean you're a lesbian," Aunt Charlotte said finally.

"I don't know," I told her. "I like guys some but I like girls more. I never thought about what to call it. I've been too busy trying to live with it. You don't want me. I'm not going home with you just so everyone can keep telling me to find a nice boyfriend to take to prom and be a good girl. I'm done with it."

"You come home with me," she said, and there was something in her voice I never expected from a grown-up sorority girl, something fierce and angry. "You've got a few months, and if you want to get the hell out of here after that I'll help."

I started to cry then. I cried hard, and I cried for a long time.

I went to live with Uncle Estlin and Aunt Charlotte and their three boys. I was lucky 'cause they treated me like they treated their sons. Eventually, Quentin could nod and shake his head, but he couldn't talk, and they sent him to live in the long-term ward at Bull Street. They decided it would be too hard for him at the house 'cause he couldn't stand noise, and with those three little ones, it was always loud. Grant was six, and you couldn't ask a six-year-old to stay quiet.

Right before I went to Princeton, the town put up a memorial for Sheriff Irwin and his deputies. No one ever figured out what happened to them—they found them dead on the kitchen floor like they'd laid down to take a nap or passed out where they stood. Five deputies, not counting the sheriff, all those men who'd talked about shutting my mouth then expected me to pour them coffee.

But I had gone into that swamp, and I had come out again.

CHAPTER TEN

2016

"What about Beau?" I asked Lila.

"What about him?" Lila's voice rasped a bit, as if it remembered the smoke. She flipped on her side and spoke to me rather than the ceiling.

"Did they find him?"

Lila pulled the tattered quilt higher. Her own great-great-aunt hadn't stitched that quilt—long ago, a Lanier woman sewed that patchwork. Lila had nothing left. "I never told anyone I saw him," Lila replied. "My brother was gone. They kept searching for awhile and then announced that he'd passed, too."

Lila's sweet Southern euphemism hurt. "You never told anyone?"

"Not until now." She closed her eyes. "I never told anyone, McKenzie, and now I did and I'm so tired."

I hated her suddenly and viciously. Why had Lila chosen me to carry the burden of her story? But she was curling up like a child, and pity broke through my anger. She'd lost everything in a sweep of terrible justice, real or imagined. I fit myself around her in that sad room, where the radiator hummed and her antique light trembled. Surrounded by beautiful Lanier family leavings, we slept.

CHAPTER ELEVEN

I left Lila with a promise to see her again. The gray morning found her hollow-cheeked, and when I said I'd call her, I wasn't sure if I'd keep my word. She kissed my cheek before I left. "Thank you, McKenzie," she told me, and it wasn't enough.

Princeton's cold bit deep, but after I slept and changed my clothes, I ventured to the library and dug deep into the stacks. It had happened. I read newspaper accounts from South Carolina's *The State*: on October 10th, 2016 ten-year-old Beau Carson had gone missing. A house fire had subsequently killed his mother and brother, along with Lower Congaree's sheriff and five of his deputies. An eighteen-year-old had pulled her brother from the flames, and they were the only survivors. The bare bones of Lila's story were true—a missing brother, a house fire. I leaned back in my wooden chair. I was alone, and my vision wobbled from hours of squinting at microfiche. It was quiet there. I listened to my heartbeat and thought of Lila hearing hers, of that swamp quiet and a terrible sense of being watched. When I whirled, no one was there. Of course, no one was there.

I thought about it for the rest of the day. I'd met Lila's dark, haunted eyes. She'd never push past it, and I didn't call her. I lost my nerve after that moment alone in the stacks.

I woke the next morning to a clear, sharp day. The sun shone bright, but I caught a dark whiff of smoke on the wind. You're imagining it, I told myself. You read too much of that microfiche.

But they were talking about it in the small shop where I grabbed my morning bagel.

A townhouse—yeah, that one around the corner there—it burnt to the ground last night, said the goateed barista as he juggled cappuccino orders. Killed a girl. A junior, he thought, dark-haired, from down South. Came in for coffee. Always polite, but sad, didn't talk much. Good tipper, though.

I threw my bagel away. I didn't need to see, but I walked there anyway.

Tape cordoned off the wet-ashed wreckage of Lila's townhouse; those beside it remained unburnt. A polluted smoke scent lingered. I clapped my gloved hand over my nose. Lila had told something meant for no one else, and that telling had called down punishment from far away.

I believed her then. I believed all of it.

Half-dazed, I stumbled back to campus and collapsed on a cold iron bench. I'd known a boy had gone missing, and I'd known a girl had pulled her brother from a burning house. I'd muddled everything else, perhaps, into desperate fiction. Lila's story provided a bulwark against the blind tyrannies of chance and small-town ignorance. It had been true for her—I'd believed that, but I'd never entertained it as anything more. I hadn't believed in a tuft-tailed panther or a boy with snake-ringed arms; I hadn't believed that something watched and waited behind moss-draped cypress trees. But if Lila's apartment had burnt—if an all-powerful awareness had punished Lila for breaking her silence—what did it mean to believe her?

If there was something in that swamp, it had reached beyond those cypresses and into Princeton's cozy cobblestone streets. It knew Lila had spoken, revealing an omniscience associated only with gods—and a demented god at that, one who honored blood deals slapped on cypress bark, who stole children, who twisted time, who remained indifferent until its interest was suddenly, viciously roused. My breath came in shallow, shuddered gasps. That burned shell of a townhouse told of a will unknowable and insane. Lila talked of justice, but there had been no justice. There was only whim, and her tale was no tragedy, but a window into the chaos that drowned us. We could simply hope to sink, never rousing that almighty entity of unreason.

I lifted my eyes to the bright-burning sun and closed them tight.

No, I decided in that red darkness behind my lids. I couldn't believe her. Lila lit the match. She'd lit it the night before, and maybe she'd lit it long ago in that house with broken shutters. There had been no blood pact, no panther, and no sick retribution. Lila had been drinking alone at the end of a bar. She'd finally unburdened herself. The barista said she always seemed sad. Lila had died by her own hand, and she'd clutched at one last, frail connection. I opened my eyes. Green and purple afterimages bloomed, floated, then faded. Lila had done it, and I was her suicide note.

Shaking, I sat in the sunshine for a long time. Lila had been right. I didn't believe her.

I refused.

AFTERWORD

A family is supposed to be a place of refuge. Centuries of stories, both fictional and true, have shown this is not a given. Yet almost all of us feel a unique sense of betrayal when we realize our kin, be they parents, siblings, or relatives, have harmed us in some way.

Betrayal is at the heart of Lila's tale. As she recounts what happened to her family to a lover she's met in a bar, we learn how much damage she, her siblings, and her mother suffered from each other as much as from the rest of their town. Lila is able to dismiss the nastiness from neighbors and from the useless cops planted in her driveway when her youngest brother, Beau, goes missing. But it's the betrayal from her family that truly breaks her heart.

Each betrayal is also worse the closer it is to her own blood. Her mother's disregard hurts less than her older brother's. Nothing hurts Lila more, though, than her own twin turning on her and trying to hurt her in the name of sibling love. Perhaps this is why Lila tells herself over and over that her brother didn't truly wish to harm her. It's the only way she can face that a literal part of her wanted to do her harm.

In the end, it's this realization that makes familial betrayal cut so deep. Our blood relatives share more than a house and a space with us. We're connected by DNA, and I believe this does something to our wiring that makes it all the harder to accept that we can be harmed by blood relatives, and more so, makes it hard to leave them behind when the harm is too much. Even when Lila eventually escapes, she carries the burden of her tale until she shares it with a stranger she slept with for a one night stand, one of the lowest-hanging fruits of intimacy possible. Even then, she isn't truly free until she goes the way of the rest of her family.

Family ties run deep, Family betrayal goes even deeper. Broadbent's story shows us how the mire of the swamp is child's play compared to the bonds of blood. After all, blood is thicker than water.

Sonora Taylor
Author of *Errant Roots*

About the Author

Elizabeth Broadbent escaped the swamps of South Carolina for the Commonwealth of Virginia, where she lives with her three sons, two cats, two dogs, flock of crows, and a very patient husband. She's the author of *Ink Vine* and *Ninety-Eight Sabers* (Undertaker Books) and *Blood Cypress* (Raw Dog Screaming Press), as well as the upcoming releases, *Tigers of Greater Antarctica* (Sley House Publications, 2026), and *Breaking Neverland* (Sley House Publications, 2026). As a freelance journalist, her work has appeared in places such as *The Washington Post*, *Time*, *Insider*, and *ADDitude Magazine*.

Reader Discussion Questions

1. Lila has very different relationships with her three brothers, especially Davis and Quentin. How does Davis treat her, and how does that contrast with the way she's treated by Quentin? Could that offer commentary about gender roles available to women in the South?

2. Lila says that, "Mama haunted our house like a ghost. She was Miss Legare County, I could've told Quentin. They took her picture and handed her roses, and she rode on top of a fire engine in the Lower Congaree Firefly Festival on the Fourth of July." She refuses to be that kind of "gray-eyed ghost." What kind of role does her mother fill, and what is Lila refusing?

3. When Lila is fourteen years old, she cuts off her hair. Why does everyone disapprove so much, and what does it mean to them?

4. When Lila objects to Miz Leonard's treatment of Beau, the old woman sniffs at the two of them and says, "Blood tells," which sends

Caroline Carson into a weeping fit. Themes of blood run through the novel, from familial blood to the blood Lila slaps on the cypress tree. How do you think they're tied together?

5. How are the police portrayed, particularly the sheriff? How do they feel about the Carson family, especially Lila and Beau, and what affects those feelings? Do you think their eventual ending is justified?

6. Beau is clearly neurodivergent, likely autistic. Why doesn't the Carson family treat him? What does it tell us about them, and how do those attitudes contribute to their undoing?

7. Lila says that her mother had "an heir and a spare and one for mama." How do each of the Carson children fulfill or refuse to fulfill those roles? How does Beau fit in—or not—and what does that mean for the story?

8. Liminal spaces are places of transition. How is the Congaree Swamp a liminal space, and how does setting function in the story?

9. Why do you think Beau runs away, and what do you think about his transformation? Is it a good or a bad thing?

10. MacKenzie refuses to believe Lila's story. She says, instead, that "Lila lit the match...and I was her suicide note." Do you agree or disagree with her? Why do you think MacKenzie refuses to believe Lila?